T0194701

THE GAME WARDENS

BOOK 3, THE GAME WARDEN'S BULLET

DAN HAYDEN

THE GAME WARDENS
BOOK 3, THE GAME WARDEN'S BULLET

iUniverse books may be ordered through booksellers or by contacting:

iUniverse
1663 Liberty Drive
Bloomington, IN 47403
www.iuniverse.com
1-800-Authors (1-800-288-4677)

ISBN: 978-1-5320-8085-2 (sc)
ISBN: 978-1-5320-8086-9 (e)

Library of Congress Control Number: 2019913182

Print information available on the last page.

iUniverse rev. date: 09/05/2019

Other Books by Dan Hayden

The Game Wardens
The Game Wardens, Book 2, Danger's Way
The Game Wardens, Book 3, The Game Warden's Bullet

DEDICATION

This book is dedicated to Harry Weinmann who has come to be a friend, teacher, and mentor. Thank-you for showing the interest in my writing and encouraging the suggested readings from certain classic novels that have helped with my creations, lectures, and book signings. Your advice and networking efforts are greatly appreciated.

REVENGE

Revenge in the mind of a tortured soul
Is a premeditated and selfish act
Heightened by vindictiveness and self-pity.

Daniel Hayden
Fish and Game Warden, Author

PREFACE

L aw enforcement officers of all kinds may experience both negative and positive feedback from citizens they may have encountered at some point in their careers. Positive feedback, which is something a good officer does not intentionally seek, may occur when a bad situation has resulted in a good ending due to the intervention of that officer. Negative feedback may occur when an officer is forced to do his job because he has either observed a wrongful act or has had reason to question a situation and follow clues or leads that may reveal a negative outcome for the perpetrator or lawbreaker.

In the event an act committed by the perpetrator has been discovered or proven to be intentional and deliberate, and the perpetrator has shown no remorse, that person is brought to justice using a system of monetary fines, community service, or incarceration, depending on the severity of the crime. These punishments, or retribution for what ever the crime may have been are what the perpetrator may deem worthy of revenge on the arresting officer.

Revenge or vendetta on an officer of the law is also a criminal act and is punishable by several times the sentence given for the original crime. Depending on the punishment, the accused may, over time, develop paranoia, or severe hatred for who or what is responsible for their current situation. These negative feelings, if allowed to go un-noticed can be very dangerous to the officer or anyone associated with him or her.

It is the intention of this book to show how the human mind can slowly deteriorate and influence one's thought process especially when coupled with time and little to no effort put forth for rehabilitation. The idea of revenge can become a compulsive drive. In line with the aforementioned paranoia and hatred, revenge can become something that must happen at all costs. The person that seeks it comes to feel that without revenge there is nothing else.

Dan Hayden
Author, The Game Warden's Bullet
July 2019

CHAPTER 1

It was a quiet evening at the Moody's cabin. The kids were up in their rooms doing homework, Peg sat by the fire reading a book, and Sam was sharpening some of his precious knives with a new gadget someone had loaned him, guaranteed to put a razor's edge on any blade. The serene atmosphere of the cabin's interior was broken by the loud ring of the home's telephone. Peg immediately shot a serious glance at her husband. Sam smiled and returned her gaze, "Don't worry, Honey. I'm not on the schedule tonight." He rose from his easy chair across from where Peg sat and walked to the kitchen to answer the phone.

"Hello?" There was a pause on the other end of the line, then a familiar voice came through the earpiece.

"Hey Sam, Lieutenant Alban here. We have to take a ride. I'll be over to pick you up in a few minutes."

Sam turned and looked back into the living room. Peg was watching his every move and listening to every word. He turned back toward the kitchen and spoke into the phone. "Uh, well I'm off tonight, LT. We kind of settled in for the night…you know?"

"I know you're off tonight, damn it. I need to talk to you about something. I'll pick you up in half an hour, we'll talk, and then I'll bring you home. It'll take about an hour… if that."

DAN HAYDEN

Sam turned back to the living room and repeated Alban's answer so Peg could hear, "Only an hour?" Peg returned Sam's statement with a flip of her hand, a disgusted glance, and a nod that meant he had her permission. Sam turned back toward the kitchen, "Okay, LT. I'll be waiting."

Lieutenant Gene Alban, Unit Commander of Thompson's Fish and Game Department drove his green Dodge pick-up truck along quietly. Sam sat in the passenger seat next to him waiting for an explanation. Finally, Alban spoke, "Remember that guy you pinched for boating under the influence (BUI) last summer?"

Sam nodded and replied, "Yeah? What about him?"

Alban shook his head, "I'm not talking about Hanks' killer. He and his bat are going away for a long time. I'm talking about the guy you arrested for BUI back in June."

Sam nodded his head in an affirmative way. "Oh yeah. He got six months in the state jail."

Alban replied without taking his eyes off the road, "Well, word on the street is that he's out and asking about your address and what your last name is."

Sam was confused. "How can that be? He got four months and another two months because he put his hands on me."

Alban slowed the truck as they came to a stop sign. He looked at Sam when the truck came to a stop. "The prosecutor plea bargained for several smaller charges because he was afraid they couldn't make the BUI charge stick. He said the light stigma test probably wouldn't be enough so they plea bargained the BUI charge away for a series of lesser charges that they knew would put him away for at least four months."

Sam shook his head in disgust. "Well, that's just wrong. The guy is going to think he can do it again and get away with a lesser charge." Sam paused and added, "Okay, so is that what you wanted to tell me?"

Alban nodded his head and added, "Partly." Then he turned his head and looked right at Sam. "I want to know how you feel about all this?"

Sam looked back out the passenger window. "Well, the guy has been in jail six times, hasn't got a car, and lives on the other side of town...and I have a wife and three children."

Alban prompted, "Go on."

Sam continued, "So, if he shows up on my property he won't leave under his own power."

Alban turned from his driving and looked back at Sam. "What are you gonna' do...shoot him?"

Sam smiled and turned to meet Alban. "I didn't say that. I said that if he shows up on my property he won't leave under his own power." The two Fish and Game officers just locked eyes for a few moments.

Alban nodded and turned back to watching the road, "Okay." Nothing else was said. Alban brought Sam home.

Peg was still sitting by the fire when Sam returned from his ride with Alban. She waited for him to put his jacket away and return to his easy chair across from where she sat. Without looking up from her book she asked, "So, what was so important that the good lieutenant had to drag you out on your night off?"

Sam glanced over at his wife, shrugged, and said, "Some guy I pinched last summer just got out of jail and rumor has it that he's asking questions about me and where I live. Routine...nothing to worry about."

Peg put the book down and looked concerned. "Sam, we have children here. It is something to worry about."

Sam pursed his lips and replied, "Alban wants to know how I'll react if the guy shows up around here."

Peg was leaning forward in her chair. "Well, what did you say?"

Sam tried to act nonchalant. "I told him the man wouldn't leave here under his own power."

Peg stood up from her chair allowing her book to fall to the floor. "Great! That's just what we need…some convict prowling around our home to get back at you…how are we supposed to live our lives? I have just about had it with this Fish and Game stuff. Now our family and way of life is threatened. It's not enough that I never know if you'll be coming back home in one piece…or at all for that matter." Peg moved her arms in the air for effect as she spoke and now started to pace in front of the fireplace.

Sam tried to calm her. He could see she was getting herself over excited. He spoke in a low but soothing tone. "Peg, sit down. You're making more of this than you need to. Yes, it's a concern but the guy is only asking questions right now. I'll get to the bottom of it but remember, convicts) are advised, especially when they're released, that vendetta against any lawmaker is weighted five to seven times the original punishment."

Peg stopped and glared at Sam. "Oh, really? …and where does that leave us, your family, after he ambushes you, and puts you in the hospital or worse, kills you?"

Sam sat motionless in his easy chair as he watched Peg rant. "Honey, we knew this kind of thing could happen when I took the job. We talked about it." Peg was still pacing back and forth before the fireplace. She stopped and looked at him but said nothing. Sam reminded her about her own judicial training. "You of all people should realize this for what it is, Peg. You have a degree in Criminal Justice for Pete's Sake."

Peg paused another moment, walked slowly up to Sam, and cradled his face with both hands. She looked into his big brown eyes and said nothing. A tear rolled down her cheek and after a few moments she removed her hands, turned and walked out of the room. Sam let her leave the room and knew the discussion wasn't over. He turned his head and looked into the fire, *Damn Alban.*

The night passed without further discussion regarding prowling convicts searching for Sam. Peg had retired for the evening and Sam spent the night in his loft in the barn.

When morning arrived, Sam showered and dressed before the rest of the family got up. He grabbed his usual coffee on the way out the door, jumped into his Ford Ranger pick-up truck and headed for the police station. On the way, he thought about his discussion with Peg the night before. Had she really had it with his Fish and Game career? She seemed pretty upset…more than usual, but the underlying concern was that she felt her family's safety was at stake. Of course, she was right to feel that way but was this just hearsay or was it a real threat? Sam decided it was only a concern for now. He couldn't live his life worrying about who was angry with him or about idle threats from low-life law breakers. This is the career he chose and Peg had helped him make the decision…she even encouraged it. Now she's fed up and wants him to quit because some loser gets out of jail and starts asking questions on the street.

Sam drove a little further trying to clear his mind of last night's tiff in the living room but Peg's words kept coming back into his head. Sam thought, *Hey, I'm the one the guy wants…not the family.* Then another thought came to mind,

Well, he could try getting back at me through my family. That is a valid concern.

The entrance to the Thompson Police Department was just ahead. Sam satisfied himself with the fact that he would do some snooping about this guy and get to the bottom of it. If it's true, maybe he'd go pick the guy up and find out his intentions personally.

Sam parked his truck and headed for the locker room. He was a bit early for shift so he suited up and went to the cafeteria to get another coffee before roll call.

He sat in his usual spot in the P.D.'s cafeteria sipping his black coffee when Lieutenant Alban walked in. He saw Sam, looked at his watch and smiled. "Hey Sam, you're a bit early, aren't you?"

"Yeah, a little. Had to get out and do a little thinking this morning."

The lieutenant poured himself a coffee and sat down next to Sam. "Would it be because of what we talked about last night?" Sam reddened a little and never lifted his gaze from the table. Alban nodded his head and asked. "How did Peg take the news?"

Sam looked up at Alban. "She wasn't too good with it, LT. I think she feels I'm endangering our family with my career. She may want me to quit."

Alban nodded again to signify he understood. "You know Sam, this is only the tip of the iceberg. The BUI pinch is nothing. That guy is just blowing smoke. He's just a regular sportsman that broke the rules, got caught, did his time, and is just blowing off steam. The guy you have to worry about is Jake Farmer."

Sam looked Alban in the eyes. "What do you mean, LT? He's still doing time, isn't he?"

Alban stood up from the table. "I wanted to see how you were going to handle a lesser scenario like the BUI pinch. Farmer got out of the hospital and has started his two-year poaching sentence. He'll be out sooner than that on parole or for good behavior, so you'd better start considering how you're going to handle it." Alban took another sip of his coffee. "If anyone has a reason to be angry, it would be Jake. Because of you, thirty-five years of law enforcement are down the drain, his pension is cancelled, and he literally has no future. Not to mention he almost died twice…also your fault."

Sam spoke up. "Wait a minute, LT. How was that my fault? I was defending myself." Sam was speaking of his attack on a poacher's camp in New Hampshire last year, of which Jake was the ring leader.

Alban sat back down. "Sam, it was a while before they could get oxygen to Jake after he had that heart attack caused by rolling around with you in the grass. The lack of oxygen caused a part of his brain to stop sending signals to his lungs to breathe. They almost lost him right there in the field that night." Alban paused a moment then added, "…and then there was the heart attack he suffered in the hospital."

Sam knew the story and merely nodded his head to indicate he understood. Then Sam added, "Well, I don't know what to say about the heart attack in the hospital. I didn't know about that."

Alban looked at Sam sternly, "I kept that one from you. Remember, Helen Woodruff came to see you and wanted to know where Jake was? It was you that suggested it was a good idea that she should see Jake since they were… romantically involved." Sam nodded his head again. Alban continued, "We're not sure what happened but Jake was still on a ventilator at the time and had a visitor that same day.

The next thing the hospital staff knew, Jake's blood pressure was through the roof and he was in the midst of a second heart attack. When the staff arrived, the visitor was gone."

Sam looked confused. "So, if Jake's in such bad shape why should I be concerned when he gets out?"

Alban smirked back at Sam. "Because he recovered from his brain and lung impairment. Seems it was temporary and with rest and the right exercise, Jake was able to make quite a recovery. When he was able, they discharged him from the hospital and started his time for the poaching incident. He'll probably be out in a year. Rumor is that his lawyer is getting them to count his time in the hospital toward his two-year sentence."

Sam stared at the table. What else could go wrong? A bad guy is out of jail and looking for him, Jake Farmer is making a comeback and could be trouble, his family may be threatened, and his wife wants him to leave his coveted Fish and Game career.

Alban could see Sam was in deep thought. He took one last slug of his coffee, placed the mug on the table and stood up again. "Sam, I'm only going to say this once. You're still new to the law enforcement game but you've been at it long enough where you've made an impact with the public. This kind of thing is something you'll get used to. How you manage it with your marriage is your business." Sam remained fixated on the table's top and said nothing. Alban tapped the table with his fingers, turned and walked out of the cafeteria.

CHAPTER 2

Jake Farmer sat behind a glass wall in the state prison visitor's room. He held a phone to his ear and spoke to his lawyer who sat on the other side of a glass partition. An armed guard stood at one end of the room and casually eyed Jake as he spoke to his visitor. "Did you get the okay to put my hospital time toward the prison sentence?" The lawyer, Thomas Dooley, looked nervous. Jake was a very foreboding man. He wanted what he wanted and wasn't patient about it.

Dooley spoke quietly into the phone that connected the two men on either side of the bullet proof glass. "I am trying, Jake. It's not easy converting a sentence like this. Consider, if you will, how the administration looks at this...a former officer of the law, who in their minds, went bad. Not a very good role model to the public."

Jake leaned in closer to the glass partition. "I don't care what the public thinks! Just get the parole board on my side."

Dooley shook his head. "You don't get it, Jake. The parole board will consider very seriously how the public might view this. You were an officer sworn to 'serve and protect.' In their eyes, you did a double cross to everyone."

Jake shifted in his seat and scooted his chair closer to the counter he sat at. "Look, Dooley. I spent six and a half months in the hospital because of Sam Moody. The bastard caused me to have a heart attack in a field, deep in the New

Hampshire woods, the night he attacked my camp. I was chained to a hospital bed for months because of him. It's not like I was having a good time…and then that bitch from New Hampshire comes to visit me and gives me another one. That is all down time that should go toward my sentence. Now you go do your lawyer stuff and get me out of here."

Dooley nodded his head in agreement. "Look, Jake. I don't want to get your hopes up but that is the tack I've taken with the board. They are taking all that into consideration. I'm doing my best."

Jake nodded back at the nervous lawyer and sat back in his chair. "You just keep trying…and don't forget to mention all those years of community service I put in. That has got to count for something."

Dooley looked back at Jake as if his client hadn't been listening to him. "Jake! You need to understand the gravity of the situation…"

Jake cut him off, stood up from his chair, and shouted into the phone. "Just get it done!"

The guard was on Jake immediately. "Okay, we're done here. Say goodbye to your visitor."

As the guard led him away, Jake turned toward the lawyer still seated behind the glass. "Just get it done, Dooley. Just get it done." The lawyer looked down at the table on his side of the glass partition and shook his head.

★★★★

CHAPTER 3

The fact that an ex con was out looking for Sam was all over the Thompson P.D. Sam wondered how that information got around so fast. He knew the lieutenant was a vault and was not accustomed to spreading rumors or leaking privileged information. Sometimes these men's men…officers of the law, Thompson's finest, could be like a bunch of old hens with their gossip.

Sam walked down the long corridor of the P.D.'s main hallway. It was a good place to gather your thoughts as one walked the long corridor, especially at this time in the morning. The BUI guy really didn't bother him. He agreed with what Alban had said…that it was just another disgruntled boater. The real threat was Farmer and what might be going through his mind.

Sam continued to walk and consider the situation. What if Farmer did have plans on getting back at Sam? What if he did show up on his property? He didn't fear the older ex-warden but he did respect his skill and experience. Sam realized Farmer could pose a problem but the question now is whether he should prepare for Jake's vengeance. It might make Peg feel more secure or it could increase her anxiety if she thought he was nervous too. He decided to do nothing for the time being. He would not relent to a man of Jake's caliber. Knowing Jake, Sam realized he would love to have

Sam and his family live their lives in that kind of continuous fear and unrest. Sam decided to watch for the signs of such a terrorist action and deal with it when and if it presented itself.

Sam reached the end of the corridor and pushed open the door to the game wardens' locker room. As usual, the room was a flurry of activity and good- natured banter. Wardens suiting up for the day's shift included sounds of Velcro tearing, buttons snapping shut, and zippers opening and closing. Several officers looked up as Sam entered the room. Sam managed a smile at the faces that looked up to greet him as he entered.

Suddenly the room became silent. There were no more muffled conversations or arguing about last night's football game. Only the sounds of men dressing in cramped quarters prevailed. Sam knew what they were thinking. It was about the recently released boater Sam had arrested for boating under the influence.

Sam picked his way between the piles of clothing, boots and equipment strewn haphazardly about the locker room. He opened his locker and started going through its contents.

"Hey, Sarge." Jack Tully, one of the new wardens, broke the awkwardness of the moment. Everyone stopped what they were doing as Jack approached Sam rooting through his locker. "Excuse me Sarge. I'm speaking on behalf of all the wardens." Tully looked back at the room of half-dressed officers. "We know about the guy that's looking for you and we just want you to know…we're on it." Sam turned from his open locker and faced the rookie warden without emotion. Tully continued, "Just so you know, we've got your back…on or off shift. Whatever you need, we're there." Sam looked at the watching faces. They all nodded in agreement to Tully's statement or gave Sam a thumbs up sign.

Sam pursed his lips and nodded at the group. "Thanks guys. I appreciate that. Hopefully, it's just a pissed off guy spouting off because he's mad about the jail time." Sam paused and looked around the room. "I really do appreciate your concern but I got this. Keep focused on your shifts and your own work for now. If I need help, I'll let you know."

Sam grabbed his uniform cap from the locker and slammed it shut. He looked back at the wardens as he turned to leave and tipped his hat. "Be safe, gentlemen."

★★★★

CHAPTER 4

S am drove around town after an early patrol in the West Hills Territory. It had been a little chilly and Sam had spent most of the morning outside his patrol car. He looked at his watch and realized it was about time for lunch. He reached down and picked up the radio mic (microphone). "Headquarters from 419."

Dispatch responded immediately. "Go ahead, 419."

"I'm in Car six, I'll be 24 for sixty." Sam had just informed dispatch in radio code he would be going to lunch and off duty for sixty minutes.

Dispatch responded, "Roger, 419. Keep your radio on. Have some activity going on by the boat launch."

Sam clicked the mic once, "419, Roger.

Sam walked into the diner and ordered a sandwich and coffee. He stared out the window and thought about the guys in the locker room that morning. *Imagine those guys thinking I'm worried about the guy I pinched for BUI.* He cocked his head to the side and raised his eyebrows a little. *Pretty thoughtful of them to let me know they have my back.*

The waitress put the food down in front of Sam and poured him a fresh cup of coffee as he continued to stare out the window. "Will there be anything else, Officer?" The waitress had been waiting for an answer.

Sam realized he was in deep thought and came back to the moment. "Uh, oh no…thanks. I'm good."

Sam Finished the lunch without even tasting what he had ordered. Still in deep thought he put some cash down on the table and started back out of the diner. When he came through the diner's doors he noticed there was the tractor part of a tractor trailer rig parked right next to his Blazer. The driver had not left much room between the tractor and the Blazer. Sam grimaced, *Jeez, he's got three parking places to his left. Why so close?*

Sam continued toward the space between the tractor's passenger side and the Blazer's driver side. The driver was in the cab door part way but bent over and rooting around under the passenger's seat as if he was searching for something.

Sam stopped just short of the cab's door, looked up and asked, "Can I help you?" The driver paused when he heard Sam's voice and straightened up so he could look down at Sam. Sam recognized him as the BUI boater recently out of jail. *There he is…Skip Barclay.*

The driver nodded his head in an up and down manner slowly. "Oh, the game warden." He grabbed hold of the cab's handles and worked his way down the steep steps.

Sam remained motionless and watched every move as the driver climbed down. The driver came over to Sam and stood before him without a word. Sam seized the opportunity and spoke first. "I understand you're looking for me, Mr. Barclay." Sam paused for effect. "Well, I'm here. What can I do for you?"

The driver began to stammer a bit. Sam continued to stare the man in the eyes. His face was stoic. The driver finally collected himself. "Uh, Yeah. I was looking for your name and address."

Still stoic, Sam asked, "Why?"

The driver was extremely uneasy. His eyes darted from side to side and he seemed a little out of breath. "Uh, well… you see…the agreement when I was released from jail was that I write the arresting officer an apology for what I did. Supposed to be part of the rehabilitation process." Sam said nothing but raised an eyebrow at the ex-inmate's statement. Barclay was feeling very awkward with Sam's silence and finally blurted, "I just needed a place to send the damn letter…ya' know?"

Sam knew the man was lying. Finally, Sam offered. "You have only one option here." Sam paused again. "…and that is to be on your way. Don't worry about me. Mind your own business and follow the rules."

The driver straightened up and looked more nervous. He knew Sam was onto him. "Okay…yes, sir. I will." Barclay paused a moment and looked about the parking lot. Then he looked back at Sam. "You know, I'm a sportsman…just like you. I don't want any trouble. I'm going." With that, Barclay turned to walk away from Sam and toward the front of the tractor.

As he approached the front of the tractor. Sam smiled and said, "Hey!" Barclay stopped and turned around. Sam continued, "Remember, vendetta is five to seven times the original sentence."

Barclay stared at Sam for a moment with a more than serious expression. Sam smiled again and tipped his uniform cap at him. Barclay turned and climbed back up into his tractor's cab. Sam watched from the ground and stepped back as the tractor backed out of its parking place. Sam smiled to himself. *Well, problem solved. Just have to wait and see what Farmer does now.*

★★★★

CHAPTER 5

Prisoner Jake Farmer sat in his bunk in cell D42. He had a cell to himself in a secluded part of the prison. The reason was for his safety. If the prison population ever got word that he had been law enforcement, his life expectancy would have been only a few months and that time would have been very uncomfortable for the ex-lawman.

Jake was sequestered to cell block D. It was an area away from the main part of the prison population. The cell block was utilized for inmates that might receive prejudicial treatment from the inmates incarcerated there because of who they were or what kind of crime they may have committed. In Jake's case, ex-lawmen were not accepted as common criminals because they had at one time carried a badge.

Jake lay in his bunk and considered everything that had happened to him in the past two years. His poaching ring had been exposed to the public, he had been suspended from the State Game Warden Unit and lost his pension of thirty-five years, was arrested in New Hampshire for carrying a nine mm pistol across state lines while suspended, and was arrested for trespassing and poaching on private property. The judge added resisting arrest and firing a weapon with intent to kill just to make sure all the other charges stuck.

Jake lay in his bunk quietly thinking to himself. *Well, it wasn't all bad. Had me a nice little romance goin' on there for a while. That stupid bitch never caught on that I was just using her for her land.* Jake was thinking of Helen Woodruff, the widow he had taken up with for the sole purpose of using her land, among other things. His blood pressure began to rise as he thought about that day in the hospital when Helen had come to visit him…and almost killed him. Whether she meant to put the fear of God into him or cause him another heart attack wasn't important. All he knew is what she did. *She'll get her's too*, Jake thought as he nodded his head on the pillow. A wicked smile crossed his weathered face as he lay in the dark staring at the ceiling of his prison cell.

The cell was designed for one man. It was the last cell at the end of a long lonely corridor. As far as Jake knew there was only one other inmate in the row and he resided at the other end of the corridor.

The cell walls and ceiling were cinder block and painted a putrid green. It was good that he couldn't see them in the darkness. A lonely lightbulb hung from the center of his cell. It was bare, with no shade attached and a pull string hung from its base in the ceiling. The cell had one tiny window on its outside wall located high near the ceiling. Even at six feet-one inch, it was impossible for Jake to look outside. It was meant merely to let the light of day into the small room…a luxury most other cells didn't have. A small toilet and sink were positioned under the tiny window at the far end of the cell. Behind his head the entire front wall of his cell included the metal bars and door that offered a view of the darkened corridor.

As Jake took in his dismal surroundings, he became more and more angry. He hated this place. He used to put would be lawbreakers in places like this and now it was he that was put here…by another lawman…Sam Moody.

He closed his eyes and began to consider his situation. How did this ever happen to him? Everything had been going so well. He had the cabin people working for him, passing him a few bucks every-time they saw him, the State Warden salary,…and now thirty-five years of pension… gone. He wondered what would happen to his house. Is the bank going to assume it? What about his beautiful truck? Where is that now?

Suddenly a vision of Sam Moody's face flashed in front of his closed eyes. Jake's blood pressure rose again, *Moody! That fucking Moody! Everything was fine until that goody two-shoes came into my life.* Jake opened his eyes. Although he remained quiet his face contorted into the snarl he was so accustomed to portray.

It's because of him I'm here. All because of that straight-laced pansy ass! I warned him way back to stay out of my affairs and he just kept coming…couldn't let anything go. Jake thought a little more about how Moody had harassed him in the last couple of years. Jake nodded his head as if to make a statement to himself, *I told him I'd kill him if he got in my way…and I will.*

★★★★

CHAPTER 6

The fall season passed and turned to a cold December. Jake Farmer was patiently waiting on his lawyer's progress with the state's judicial system. He kept himself busy in the prison library studying guerrilla warfare, and Marine sniper techniques of World War II. He requested permission for time in the prison library every chance he got. It got to be a running joke among inmates. "Hey Jake, what are you doing…writing a book?"

Jake kept a notebook that he scribbled the more noteworthy sections into and studied topographical maps of the forested areas around Thompson. Although he was intimately familiar with Thompson's forests and waterways, he began to train himself to look at those same areas in a different way. Jake looked for hideouts, cliffs, swamps, darkened pine forests, and any other part of the area's natural terrain that he could use to his advantage. If he was going to ambush and trap Sam Moody, the element of surprise coupled with the advantage of what the worst of what the environment could offer, would give him the advantage. Sam was an experienced outdoorsman and had also been trained in forest survival techniques. Jake knew full well he was going to need a fool proof plan in order to get the jump on another warden…especially Sam Moody.

First, Jake looked for Moody's vulnerabilities. The first thing that came to mind was his family. Sam was a family man first and placed his wife and children above all else. That would be factor number one in the plan. Another was that Sam had a good heart. Even with all his training, he'd always given the other party the benefit of the doubt. He was too trusting. *Ah*, Jake thought. *Now that's something I can use to start my plan.* Jake sat back in the prison library's chair, smiled and put his hands behind his head. *I'll use all the good parts of Sam's personality against him. Just like luring a turkey in during hunting season.*

Jake's daydreaming was interrupted by a voice from behind. "What are you working on there, Jake?" Jake was surprised from behind and shocked out of his daydreaming. He turned in his chair to see the head corrections officer of his cellblock standing behind him. It was Lieutenant Lanahan.

Jake straightened up, dropped his hands to the table, and turned back to his research. "Ah, just looking over some of my old haunts. You know, once a game warden always a game warden."

The lieutenant stepped closer to the table and peered over Jake's shoulder. "Topographical maps, Connecticut River bottom charts…hmmm. What's all this, Jake?"

Jake remained cool and was ready to lie. He spoke quietly…almost a murmur. "Guess I'm just missing some of the of the places I used to frequent…on patrol. Stays in your blood…ya'know?"

The lieutenant raised his eyebrows and pursed his lips as he looked down at Jake. Lanahan reached down and flipped the thick book of topographical maps closed. He finished the gesture by laying his open hand down on the book, palm side down, and leaned into Jake's space. Jake was once again taken aback by the lieutenant's gesture. Lanahan offered a weak smile and said, "Unfortunately, you're never going to have to look at any of this stuff again. Your days as a warden are over…forever." With that, the lieutenant offered another weak smile while he straightened up and tipped the brim of his uniform cap at Jake. "That's all over for you, Jake." Lieutenant Lanahan paused to see if Jake was going to respond to the moment. When he saw Jake was indifferent to his actions and statements, he nodded his head once and walked away.

Jake didn't even watch the lieutenant leave. To do so would have been an act of defiance. Instead, he just lowered his gaze to the closed book on the table. Inside Jake was fuming. *Sonuvabitch knows he's safe in here with all his little guard buddies to protect him. He knows I gotta' take his shit when and if he wants to give it to me. Well, all that will change soon. I can put up with that puke for now.* A hint of a small smile crossed Jake's face as reached to re-open the book.

★★★★

CHAPTER 7

The days were growing colder and December turned to January. Thompson was known to get its fair share of snow each year, usually after the beginning of January. It seemed as if the last ten years had been colder by comparison of the last thirty but the little hill town had always been prepared for nature's worst. It depended on how one looked at it. Of course, the increased snow was at best, an inconvenience, but allowed the winter sports to thrive which was one of Thompson's supporting industries.

Winter enhanced revenue from tourists that skied, snowshoed, or ice fished. The little town depended on that support because it only sported one textile factory. The small mom and pop businesses that dotted the area were not enough to keep everyone in work or help with the town's tax base.

Thompson was noted for its ice fishing. The region's ice anglers had been anxiously awaiting the cold so the town's rivers, lakes and ponds could freeze to a safe thickness that allowed the sport.

Fish and Game Captain John Fletcher stood in front of his office window with his hands clasped behind his back and stared at the lightly falling snow as it covered the forests across the way. He took a puff on his corncob pipe and blew a smoke ring at the glass.

The Captain was a quiet, unassuming man. He liked to watch a situation develop before offering an opinion or statement. When asked for advice he generally took his time in answering and when he did answer, it was after some careful, deep-seated consideration. Fletcher was a big man at six feet one inch tall and in considerably good condition for a man approaching sixty. Once an active warden, the hard, chiseled cut of a younger man's appearance was slowly rounding out to a softer, not-so-severe look. The serious, stoic signature of a law enforcement personality was still present, but not as apparent. Several years of riding a desk had contributed to that as well.

His years of experience on the State's Fish and Game Unit had not only earned him a wealth of knowledge in his professional career regarding law enforcement and rescue operations but also a great understanding for his men and for their needs as officers.

Fletcher nodded his head and turned toward his desk to pick up the phone. The phone beeped and his secretary, Maggie answered. "Yes, Sir."

Fletcher blew another puff of smoke past the phone. "Maggie, get Lieutenant Alban in here. I want to discuss winter training for my boys…Ice and Cold Water Training to be specific."

Maggie sat just outside the Captain's office in a little cubicle of her own. She looked out of her window as Fletcher spoke and acknowledged the falling snow. "Okay, Captain. I'll call him right now." Fletcher nodded and hung up.

When Lieutenant Gene Alban approached Fletcher's door the captain had been standing in front of the window again, his back to the door. Alban Knocked once and

Fletcher turned to face his guest. Alban spoke first, "Hi Cap. You wanted to see me?" Fletcher looked at the floor while nodding his head and motioning for Alban to come and sit.

Once Alban was seated, Fletcher sat in his big leather padded chair and reached into one of his desk drawers. He pulled out a notebook with the words ICE and COLD WATER TRAINING boldly printed across the cover. Fletcher tossed the notebook onto the desk in front of Alban.

Alban glanced at the book and looked back at Fletcher. "When do you want it, Cap?"

Fletcher had been watching Alban and took another puff from his pipe before answering. "There's been steady cold for six weeks now...colder than usual years. Ice should be thick enough. Get that damn fire department to get out to one of the ponds and cut a hole in it. You're going to have to work with their Chief to coordinate the classroom part with a specialist from New Hampshire. I want them in the water that night...as soon as the classroom part is over."

Alban's mouth dropped. "I have to work with the fire department's Chief?"

Fletcher put his right hand up as if to say stop. "Don't want to hear it, Gene. Orders from above. The firefighters will be taking the class along with our boys. One big class. Just do it." Fletcher put his head down and started to busy himself with other paperwork on his desk. After a moment he looked up questioningly at the bewildered lieutenant. "Call me when you get it organized." Fletcher turned his attention back to his paperwork and went back to reading.

Alban stood up and said, "Okay, I'll get right on it Cap," and left the room.

Lieutenant Alban returned to his own office and paced the floor in front of his desk. He was upset at having to work with the fire department on something that traditionally and historically were the responsibilities of the Fish and Game department. It was becoming all too obvious that the fire department was forcing their way into Fish and Game business…and for good reason. There were fewer structural fires these days due to better construction methods and building materials, in company with stricter codes, reducing the frequency of structural fires. Of course, there were the occasional brush and forest fires that threatened Thompson's recreational revenues, but new fire technology and response times also reduced that threat which was pretty much a seasonal thing anyway.

Alban knew that the fire department had to justify its cause…it's reason for existence, and if there was no frequency of fires how would the city's budget justify new equipment and firefighter's salaries? Alban stopped dead in his tracks as he realized the answer. The fire department was adding medical emergencies and river rescue to their responsibilities. Emergencies occur night and day as a result of traffic accidents, industrial and civilian accidents, and sports events. It now became clear why fire trucks were dispatched with an ambulance at a routine house call. Alban stared at the floor and thought, *Now, they're going to try to take the rescue business. They have no familiarity with the rivers or how to negotiate them.* Alban shook his head as he began to pace again. *It's one thing to get an ambulance to a scene and administer medical aid but rescue practice out in the middle of a dark, cold, angry river is quite something else.*

The angry lieutenant paced a little more but every time he came up with a reason why the fire department shouldn't be involved, he heard Captain Fletcher's voice in the back of his head, *Orders from above. Just do it.*

Alban sat down frustrated and picked up the phone. "Maggie, get Dispatch to call Sergeant Moody in here. He's on patrol in the West Hills Territory right now. Tell him the Unit Commander wants see him, ASAP." Maggie acknowledged and hung up. Alban slammed the phone back down into its cradle.

★★★★

CHAPTER 8

S am Moody had just finished a snowshoe patrol around the base of the West Hills Territory and was stowing the last of his equipment into his patrol Blazer, Car 6. "Headquarters to 419." The call came in over Sam's portable radio that hung from his duty belt. It was snowing hard at the base of the hills and the wind was picking up.

Sam slammed the hatchback's Blazer closed, unclipped the portable and keyed the mic. "West Hills,…at the base. Call you back in two."

Dispatch acknowledged, "Roger that."

Sam climbed into the cruiser and turned the ignition on. The cruiser's radio came to life as the status lights illuminated and began their system checks. Sam wiped the snow from his coat and threw his fur lined skull cap onto the passenger seat. The hat badge pinned to the folded fur visor on it's front clinked as it struck against the seatbelt. He blew a large sigh of relief as the vapor from his breath immediately began to freeze against the inside of the windshield. Sam picked up the mic and keyed it once, "419…Headquarters."

Dispatch responded, "419, return to 22 (headquarters). Unit Commander wants a word."

Sam held the mic near his mouth with his finger off the key and stared out of the snowy windshield. *What's up now?*

You think they could have made the call before I got wet and cold. Nothing out here anyway. Another GOA (Gone on Arrival). Sam had been sent to check out a hunting party that was reported as hunting too close to private property boundaries. Sam shrugged his shoulders and keyed the mic again, "419, roger. Returning to 22. ETA is 30 minutes."

CHAPTER 9

S am parked Car 6 and walked into police headquarters through the ambulance bay. He was soaked from the blowing snow and the snowshoe patrol, and wanted to shake himself off before going to see the Unit Commander, Lieutenant Alban. He removed his gloves and parka and hung them on the bay wall near the entrance to the police department administrative offices. He looked down at his jungle boots. They were wet and muddy. He wondered if he should go to the locker room first and put on his other pair and quickly dismissed the thought. He reminded himself that Alban ordered him in from patrol and was probably expecting him to be a little soggy. Sam smiled to himself and opened the door to the PD's Administration area and headed for the Unit Commander's office.

Lieutenant Alban sat at his desk awaiting Sam's arrival. *Where in hell is that Moody?* He glanced at his watch, *I heard him radio in an ETA of thirty minutes. It's been forty-five.* As if on cue there was a knock at the door. Alban sat up straight in his desk chair, "Come."

The door opened and a damp game warden stood in the doorway before being asked to sit. "You wanted to see me, LT?"

Alban motioned for Sam to come in. "Have a seat, Sergeant. I want to discuss some winter training with you."

Sam appeared a little surprised and thought it was a little strange to be called in from a patrol to discuss training.

"Okay, LT. We're between hunting seasons right now. Do you want me to go over some game laws for the upcoming deer and turkey season?"

Alban had his head down as he looked at the ICE and COLD WATER TRAINING notebook. He picked up the book and tossed it across the desk. "I want you to get the Marine Division together and brief them as soon as possible. Next Tuesday night you guys have to take a class on this. A specialist in rescue tactics from New Hampshire will be the instructor."

Sam picked up the notebook. It was a regular size notebook but about an inch thick. He looked up at Alban. "Okay LT, but with all due respect, I have to ask why Sergeant Stafford isn't doing this? It is, after all, his section now." Sam was gently reminding Alban he had chosen Sergeant Tom Stafford in lieu of him last year for the Marine Sergeant position.

Alban looked up and right into Moody's eyes and with loaded sarcasm said, "Oh, I'm sorry Sergeant. Did that hurt your feelings?" Moody straightened in his chair and his face flushed a bit…although it was un-noticeable since his cheeks were still red from the cold. Sam began to say something but Alban cut him off. "Sam, I had to make choices. Right now, Stafford is down with the flu and Fletcher wants this done ASAP. You are Skipper Certified and have more experience anyway."

Sam was a little more guarded now. Alban had said it. He was asking Sam to lead the ICE and COLD WATER rescue training because Stafford was sick. "Okay, LT. I'll get a memo out tonight to the guys and schedule a briefing for tomorrow night. Once I get confirmation of their attendance, I'll revise their schedules for the training on Tuesday evening."

Alban nodded his head. "Okay, Sam…and one more thing." Moody stood from the chair. "You are going to be working with the Fire Department on this. They'll be in class with you and your men. Make me proud."

Sam looked at the book and then back at Alban. "Okay, LT." Alban nodded at the door and Sam left the room.

— — —

The following evening as Sam was about to enter the warden's locker room, he stopped and paused before opening the door. Loud, energized chatter and good natured laughing and joking emanated from behind the door. The wardens had each received a memo from Sergeant Moody to attend a briefing on Ice and Cold Water Training. The memo explained the training was scheduled for next Tuesday evening and would be conducted at the Thompson Fire Station. Also, attendance is mandatory for all Marine Division officers and recommended for wardens whose territories included bodies of water.

Warden Tully had started the conversation by ribbing another new warden, Josh Cummings. "Hey Josh. I don't think they're going to let you participate until you learn how to swim."

Cummings threw a towel at his locker mate and retorted, "Well, I guess you're out too…being afraid of the water and all." The towel came flying back rolled up in a ball. Marine Corporal Frank Beech watched and laughed along with everyone else but stayed out of the verbal assaults.

One of the marine officers noticed Beech's lack of participation and decided to include him. "Hey Corporal!

Remember, propellers aren't good on ice. Don't want to damage another one of those and cause the department another couple of C-notes." The officer was referring to a propeller Beech had damaged last summer while trying to position the department 's main patrol boat, Marine One, for a photograph for the regional newspaper. The bantering spread to the rest of the locker room and led to a lot of good-natured jokes and needed belly laughs.

The raucous behavior was due in part to the boredom of the winter months and because of some apprehension about what they had heard about the specialized training and didn't know what to believe or expect, so they made jokes about it. At least no one made any negative remarks about having to work with the fire department. Sam took a step back, turned, and walked away. *I'll let them have their fun... blow off some steam for now.* Sam looked at his watch and decided to go have a coffee and wait for the locker room to clear before changing into his civies.

★★★★

CHAPTER 10

T he next evening Sam walked into the police department's training room. It was Thursday and Sam knew some of the wardens were not going to be working the weekend. The guys milled around the room talking and some just sat looking bored and awaiting the inevitable.

Sam walked up to the podium and the room became quiet as everyone took their seats. Sam looked out into the room of wardens and began, "Good evening gentlemen. Thanks for coming. I know some of you have been on shift all day and need to get home, and some of you are just beginning a shift, so I'll make this short. We have been ordered by our captain and invited by the Fire Department brass to attend a class on Ice and Cold Water rescue techniques." There was some murmuring and grumbling about the room so Sam stifled it. "Okay, can it. I know what you're thinking and I'm right there with you but the Fire Department is making an attempt to work with us so let's try to play nice."

One of the wardens spoke up. "Has this got anything to do with the fact that the Fire Department just purchased a new hovercraft for rescues?" Immediately the room came alive with loud opinions and statements…some harsh, some matter-of-fact.

Sam took a deep breath and answered the question. "Of course, it does. It doesn't mean they will be taking the rescue business away from us though. Look at it as if we're getting more help." More grumbling could be heard but now at a much lower volume. Sam let it pass and paused for a few moments. When the room was quiet again, Sam continued. "I want you guys at the fire department at 1830 hours (6:30 PM). Be early if anything. We don't want to give those guys anything to complain about. We'll be in the training room at the south end of the station, just left of bay one." Sam paused and looked about the room. "Any questions?"

One hand rose. It was rookie warden Jack Tully. "Yeah, I have one, Sarge. What do we bring? I mean are you handing out books…do we bring note books?"

Sam smiled and held up the Ice and Cold Water text book. It was notebook size and about one inch thick. "You will bring one of these with you and a pen for taking notes. I'll give each of you a book as you leave. Have it read before the training on Tuesday night." Audible groans and various expletives floated about the room. Sam smiled as he looked down at the podium trying to stifle a snicker. He looked back at the group of wardens and said, "Hey, I told you…I'm right there with you. I have to read it too. I'm not happy either but we have to get it done." Sam paused and leaned forward over the podium for effect. "This is important gentlemen. Read it and be ready. You know the fire department guys would just love it if they could one-up you." The men suddenly became serious. Sam stood there a few seconds, looked at the group of wardens and smiled. "Have a nice weekend." "Okay, dismissed." Sam stood by the training room door and passed out the Ice and Cold Water text books as his men left the room.

— — —

Sam stood in the foyer to Thompson's one and only fire station. It was a fairly new building made of brick and housed four fire engines, and now a hovercraft. The station was comfortable and dimly lit since only a skeleton crew was on duty for the evening. Every now and then, static of a garbled radio transmission or a tone of some sort radiated from the station's communication center. The fire engines sat dormant in their bays shiny and organized. They gave the impression of huge, stately beasts of some sort ready to spring into action on command.

He looked at his watch. It was 1815 hours…fifteen minutes before the scheduled training class. Almost all of the scheduled firemen had arrived and sat in their chairs. Sam looked back out at the dark and quiet parking lot. *Damn guys have to wait until the last minute. I told them to be early, if anything.*

The firefighters noticed Sam awaiting the arrival of his men. One of them decided to bring it to everyone's attention. "Hey Sarge, maybe your Fish and Game guys are just afraid of cold water." The room of about twenty firefighters exploded with laughter.

Moody was in no mood for such sarcasm, especially from a subordinate. He turned and walked into the room. He stopped right in front of the outspoken fireman's desk to get everyone's attention. The room became silent. Now that he had everyone's attention, Sam lifted one leg up and sat on the edge of the outspoken fireman's desk so he was looking right down at him. The fireman became extremely uncomfortable with the close quarters between them. Sam kept a straight face and looked down into his eyes. "Are you a wise ass?" The fireman, besides being mortified in front of his peers, didn't know what to say, so he said nothing and looked down at the desktop. Sam waited a few awkward moments before continuing. Then he leaned forward and softly said, "Let's try and play nice tonight. I don't like sarcasm but I am touched that you're worried about my men." Sam sat on the desk a few moments longer and when the fireman remained quiet, Sam nodded his head and stood up from the desk. There was murmuring from the back of the room but nothing Sam could understand. He walked back out to the Foyer.

Cars and pickup trucks began to enter the fire station's parking lot. As wardens began heading toward the station entrance, Sam opened the door with one hand and pointed at his watch with the other. The last man through the door was Jack Tully. "It's just 1830 now, Sarge."

Sam smirked at the man, "…and you're not early, Rookie."

Sam sat and listened to the training. The instructor was extremely good. He was on loan from a federal organization specializing in rescue and safety techniques. The instructor kept the class interested and motivated and showed a few disheartening videos toward the end where children were the victims. That seemed to grab the attention of everyone in the room. It drove the point home as to the importance of the topic.

When the lights came on, everyone was still sitting upright and attentive. They had had a great two-hour lecture with some profound videos to make the training come together. Sam considered it some of the best training he'd ever had. He stood from his desk and made for the door. The rest of the wardens followed. As he exited the training room entrance, Chief Russo stood leaning against one of the fire trucks. He smiled at Sam and said, "Where are you going, Sergeant?"

Sam looked behind him. All ten of his men were right there. Sam smiled back. "Oh Hello, Chief. We're going home." He felt something wasn't right. Sam paused and asked, "Training is over…isn't it?"

The chief stepped away from the fire truck. "Not quite. Now, you gotta' go do it."

★★★★

CHAPTER 11

The Game Wardens piled into a narrow crew space within the confines of the big hook and ladder fire truck. There was what could only be described as a long tunnel about four feet wide and five high that extended from the rear of the truck up to the driver's cab area. Bench seats lined one side of the tunnel.

Some of the firemen rode with the game wardens, others rode in a separate auxiliary fire vehicle. Sam looked down the row of men. Everyone looked glum. It was nine o'clock PM, 27 degrees F, and the wind was at fifteen miles per hour with snow flurries. The men knew it was cold and the thought of crawling out onto a frozen pond was disconcerting. They knew they were going to have to go in the water but weren't sure of what to expect.

They had just spent the last two hours in a nice, warm training room at the Thompson fire station and were ready to go home to their families. The Chief's unannounced practical part of the training had been a complete surprise, suddenly and without warning, and no details were given about what they were expected to do. The surprise practical was just like…or as close to, a real rescue situation as possible.

Sam stood hunched over holding onto a handrail that ran along the upper part of the tunnel wall. Rookie warden

Jack Tully looked nervous so Sam tried not to notice. Tully finally stood up and leaned into Sam's ear. "Where are we going, Sarge?"

Sam met Tully's worried gaze and looked away with no expression, "To one of the bodies of water around here… probably the town pond."

Tully's mouth dropped open. "Do you think they'll really make us go in the water? It's way below freezing tonight."

Sam looked back at Tully and in an even but understanding tone said, "Jack, relax. This is what we do. It'll be like this in a real rescue situation. You won't know what you have to deal with until you get there. Just be ready for anything." With that said, Tully nodded his head and sat back down.

Sam smiled to himself. *I don't want to go into that damn cold water either but I can't let the guys know that. I'm going to have to make it look like it's just another routine practice.* He knew his men would be watching his face for some kind of reaction so he concentrated on maintaining an expression of indifference. He was their sergeant and was going to do whatever it took to ensure the guys were comfortable.

Within the confines of the narrow crew space, the men could feel the truck lurch from side to side whenever it initiated a turn. Since there were no windows, they could only guess at where they were in the dark, cold town of Thompson. Finally, the fire truck came to a stop. The truck's cab door opened and Chief Russo climbed up the stairway and ducked his head into the tunnel. "Here we are, gentlemen. I hope you're ready to go for a swim." He offered a wicked smile, almost a sneer, then turned and exited the truck. There were groans and choice words muttered throughout the inside of the fire truck.

Suddenly, the rear doors behind Sam opened. Firemen stood outside waiting for its temporary occupants to come out. Sam stepped out of the truck first and down to the gravel parking lot. He knew where he was immediately and looked to his left. It was the Thompson town pond. It was frozen solid, and out in the middle, there was a large triangular hole cut in the ice. Each leg of the triangle was about eight to ten feet long.

The Chief made sure to have the truck's spotlight aimed at the ice hole so the participants could see it. *Aw shit*, he thought. *I really don't want to go in that friggin' cold water.* Chunks of ice floated in the man-made hole that made it appear even colder. Snow flurries illuminated by the truck's spot light gave the whole scenario an uncomfortable atmosphere.

He looked back at his men who had been standing around him in the parking lot. They were watching his face. *I can't let them know I'm as nervous about doing this as they are.*

Just then Chief Russo walked by the group of wardens. Sam spoke up. "Hey Chief. I'd like Fish and Game to go in first."

Chief Russo nodded his head at Sam. "Okay, Sergeant."

Sam couldn't help but notice the icy stares from his wardens. He looked back at the Chief. "I'll go first."

The Chief glanced over at a few of the firefighters huddled by the rear of the truck. "Suit him up."

Sam was brought back into the warm fire truck to get suited up. He was ushered to a space just forward of the tunnel and behind the truck's cabin and told to take off everything except his tee shirt and jeans. Socks could stay.

Two firefighters helped him put the dry suit on. It was a one-piece job that included booties, mittens, and hood.

There was no chatter as the firefighters helped him into his suit, just a lot of silent observation from the wardens. The suit was made of a thick neoprene material, impervious to water, hence the name dry suit. Water could not get to the wearer since the suit completely encapsulated its occupant. The only open skin was that of his face from just above the eyebrows to just below his lower lip. Once the hood was pulled over his head, one of his valets said, "Let's get him outside before he starts to sweat too much."

Sam walked to the end of the tunnel and stepped out of the rear of the truck to a waiting Chief Russo. "He's ready Chief."

The chief smiled at Sam and said, "Burp 'em." Immediately the fireman on Sam's right ran the inside of his right forearm along the length of Sam's body from his waist to his upper chest. A whoosh of warm air audibly exited Sam's suit from just under his chin followed the slap of a flap that hung off the side of Sam's hood. The same fireman quickly secured the flap over Sam's face where it joined a Velcro tab on Sam's left cheek. Another fireman attached a carabiner to a loop on Sam's chest that was attached to one hundred feet of line. The coiled line was looped around Sam 's neck and hung diagonally across his body so that it rested on his opposite hip. He was ready to begin his rescue.

Chief Russo pointed to the hole in the ice about eighty feet offshore. "Go get him, Sergeant." Sam looked out over the ice. There was a man in the ice hole, also wearing a dry suit awaiting Sam's arrival. The scene was ominous. The fire truck's floodlight was trained on the hole in the black ice causing a spotlight effect that made the surrounding area completely dark. Sam could only see the illuminated path to his victim highlighted by thousands of bright white snow flurries that seemed to dance in the beam of light.

Sam's wardens stood on the frozen shoreline watching their sergeant as he ambled down to the edge of the frozen pond. He looked and walked like an astronaut in a bulky space suit carrying a lot of rope.

When Sam got down to the ice, he checked that his carabiners were closed and got down on his hands and knees to begin his crawl out to the victim in the ice hole. By crawling on all fours he reduced the impact of his total weight on the ice spreading it over four contact points instead of one for each footstep.

It was slow going and Sam could feel the line over his shoulder pay out as he moved forward. A shore party of six firefighters held the other end of Sam's lifeline. As Sam approached the ice hole, he saw his victim clearly for the first time. It was a fireman completely immersed in the hole but resting his forearms on the hole's ice edges to keep his body in one place. The ice was about six inches thick and could have easily supported a man and a vehicle if necessary, but for practice, the conditions seemed to be ideal.

Sam edged up to the hole and the fireman continued to look straight ahead and ignore his presence. Sam said nothing as he lowered himself over the ice hole's edge and into the freezing water. He felt the pond's water pushing against his dry suit but not entering. The suit made him so buoyant he had to keep hold of the hole's edge to keep from flopping around. It was also warm in the suit. Even though he wore nothing but a tee shirt and jeans under the suit, he worked up a sweat.

Sam worked his way over to the supposed victim. Neither man said a word. Sam inched up behind the submerged firefighter and reached around him to clip his carabiner to the fireman's chest. The man was huge. Sam couldn't get his arm around the man's girth. He thought, *They probably picked the biggest fireman they could for this drill.* Sam pulled his right arm back and with one great effort, swung it around the man's torso. In the dark, he felt for the clip on the fireman's dry suit. *There it is,* he thought, and in one quick slash with the carabiner, pulled it across the loop and heard it snap closed.

Sam was already in position behind the supposed victim and was now connected to him by a tether from the victim's chest to a clip on Sam's suit...also at the chest. Sam looked to the shore party holding the end of the land line that he had dragged out to the hole. One signal from him and they would all pull at the same time. He looked back at his victim and remembered the training from earlier that night. *Okay, the shore party has the line that's hooked to me, and I'm hooked to this giant. Time to give them the signal and push up on his butt when the line goes taut.* Sam reached up over his head and tapped the top of his hood three times. He felt the line go taut and pushed up on the victim's butt with his left hand to get the motion started. Sam and the victim fireman flew out of the ice hole like a rocket.

The shore party, seeing the result of their effort took the opportunity to have some fun. They pulled with all their might dragging Sam and his rescued fireman across the frozen pond. The two men tumbled and slid along the ice as the shore party reeled them in. Sam found himself laughing as he was dragged along with his victim. He felt relief and satisfaction. In the background along the frozen edge of the pond, onlookers, wardens and firefighters clapped and cheered. Chief Russo interrupted the celebration and shouted into the cold, night air, "Okay, let's go. Who's next?" To his amazement, Sam heard the rest of the wardens arguing. Everyone wanted to be next.

Sam smiled to himself as he stood up from the ice and felt confident not only about himself but also that his men were no longer worried. Now they were eager to participate.

★★★★

CHAPTER 12

T he holidays had come and gone and February was fast approaching. Jake Farmer sat in his prison cell reading a book from the prison library. The book was entitled Tracking and Trapping Techniques for Large Animals. Jake tossed the book to the end of his bed and rubbed his eyes. It was getting late. He craned his neck so he could get a glimpse of the clock at the end of the corridor. *Nine o'clock. They'll be turnin' out the lights in an hour. Better turn in early tonight. Got that meeting with Dooley in the morning. Hope that son of a bitch got me a grant on my hospital time.*

Jake lay back on his pillow and stared up at the ceiling. The cell block was quiet. A lone ceiling light hung at each end of the long corridor and provided a subdued illumination but no shadows. Some of that light spilled into his little cell but not enough. He used a pull string that hung from the ceiling at the center of the cell to activate the one miserable bare light bulb that serviced his living space. In keeping with the dim lighting, the cell was cool, just a notch above uncomfortable.

Eventually, Jake's thoughts turned to his arrest in New Hampshire. He hoped the judicial system would consider the time he was hospitalized as part of his sentence. His feeling was that Sam Moody was responsible for putting him there and that should be considered. *I can't see why they*

wouldn't count my time in the hospital as part of my sentence.
Hell, It's Moody's fault I'm in here. He was the one that caused me
to have that heart attack in the middle of that New Hampshire
field two years ago,…attacking me like he did. It's his fault I ran
up that huge hospital bill…God only knows what that must have
been after a year of guarded care…not to mention all the machines
they had me hooked up to.

As Jake thought about all of the reasons for his stay in
the state penitentiary his right fist continued to pound the
mattress. With each thought he pounded the mattress a
little harder. He felt the frustration and the anger, and in his
warped mind felt that it was everyone else's fault for getting
in his way. One of the guards stationed at the end of Jake's
corridor heard the pounding and came to investigate. "Hey,
Jake. What in hell are you doing to your mattress?"

The sudden appearance of the guard at Jake's cell door
shocked him back to reality. He never realized what he had
been doing with his fist. Jake looked up at the guard and
then down at his fist. Embarrassed, he replied sheepishly.
"Oh sorry, Officer. I was just thinking of one of my favorite
tunes. Playin' it out in my head…trying to keep time I
guess."

The guard smirked at Jake. "Well, knock it off. It's
almost lights out anyway."

In a few minutes the lights dimmed across the cell block
just as the guard had promised. An indistinguishable and
unemotional voice came over the public address system.
"Lights out. Lights out. Quiet hours are now in effect." Jake
listened to the broadcast and went back to considering how
much of his dilemma was Sam Moody's fault. The same
thoughts badgered him day and night to the point where he
knew he had to do something about it. Studying the terrain
of Moody's patrol area, and planning ambushes in all kinds

of scenarios began to consume most of Jake's waking time. Planning the way in which he would take revenge seemed to alleviate some of his anxiety, but still wasn't enough. His whole life seemed to be centered around the man most responsible for putting him in this god-awful place.

Jake pulled the blanket from his bed up around his shoulders. He was cold and alone in this dark place. The only person that came to visit was his lawyer, Tom Dooley. His sister Carol wrote letters once in a while but hadn't seen him since his hospital stay. She blamed Jake for getting her husband Billy Jaggs, shot that night in the field. Because of that one night and one bullet from Tom Stafford's rifle, Billy had lost the use of an arm. The bullet had smashed his shoulder joint to bits resulting in excessive nerve damage and other musculoskeletal problems. Once out of prison, Billy would be very limited as to what kind of work he would be able to do, if he could find work at all. His reputation was ruined as well.

The newspapers had splashed the whole ordeal statewide. The headline said, Law Enforcement Officer Caught Poaching. Information from the testimonies of captured ring members became public knowledge. The one that topped it off was that from his would-be girlfriend, Helen Woodruff. Her testimony spared no detail as to what Jake did under false pretenses. That testimony put the lid on who Jake really was as a person.

Jake continued to lay in the dark thinking about all the people who had worked to put him in this place. He began with Helen Woodruff. *That Helen. She really turned on me. Okay, at first, I was just using her for the use of her land, but after a while it was actually the closest thing I'd ever had to a real relationship. Then she comes to see me in the hospital and damn near kills me.* Jake let his mind wander a little. He knew he was getting himself worked up. As he began to relax his thoughts drifted back to his situation. He began to think about Sam Moody again. *I gotta' plan his ambush carefully. He's too good in the woods so I'm going to have to really lean on the element of surprise. What can I do to really hurt this guy?* Jake considered several areas in which he could hurt Sam with maximum impact. Then he realized, *His family is what is most precious to him, of course…and I hear he's got a dog now… with only three legs at that. Hmmn. If I can distract him enough by doing something to his family or that stupid dog, that might just give me the edge I need.*

Jake began to smile as he lay in his dark prison cell. He had the beginning of a plan…just an idea right now, but a beginning, and the idea suited him. His revenge on Sam was about to come together. Jake knew he couldn't write any notes down or keep a diary. The guards would find that in no time. He'd have to plan this whole thing in his head and memorize it. All the better, he decided. By the time he got to execute it, he'd have the plan down pat. Before he closed his eyes again, one more thought came to him. *I'll get those buddies of his, Tom Stafford and Pat James too. They hang around like they're brothers or something. Stafford is going to pay for shooting Billy and I'm going to torture that James for pushing me around that time in the P.D. in front of the guys.* As Jake began to fall asleep he remembered Pat James sighting in on him that night in the field. *Bastard puts a laser sight on my forehead…Academy puke!* Jake was asleep.

★★★★

CHAPTER 13

The month of February brought its usual effects but temperatures were unusually cold. All of the major bodies of water had frozen over and had grown thicker than years past. Even the faster areas of the Connecticut River had partially frozen over. The ice fishermen were happy about the ice but the extra inches were a little inconvenient. The ice anglers brought their ice augers out to their favorite holes but the frustration of having to re-cut the ice hole before they could fish became more and more frustrating as the winter droned on. Due to the extra inches of hard ice, more time was required to drill or re-drill old holes.

Sam had just left the Thompson P.D in his assigned cruiser Car six, for an early morning patrol. He smiled to himself as he headed west toward the Connecticut River. He glanced up at the dawning sky. It was still fairly dark below the clouds and the sun was rising out of the east casting a light red hue along their base. The same cloud layer was light grey near it's flattened top exposing a silvery corona against a brightening blue sky above. Sam enjoyed the spectacle as the beginning of another brisk winter day greeted him.

He looked at his watch and then over at his dog Traveller, seated next to him in the passenger seat. Traveller was a black lab Sam had rescued about a year ago from a train trestle spanning the Connecticut River. He'd lost a hind leg to a train but was fully recovered and thanks to the Moody children and good medical care, had resumed a normal way of life. He had turned out to be a great addition to the family and was very protective of the Moodys.

It was 0615 hours or in laymen terms, 6:15 in the morning. Traveller sat bolt upright and faced front, as if he were a human passenger…or partner, looking through the cruiser's windshield. Sam smiled and thought, *the perfect partner…understands what I want, smart, quiet, and dependable.* Sam had been taking Traveller with him on patrol more than usual lately. It was company for Sam and it gave the dog something to do all day. Walking through the snow was a lot of work so Traveller tended to follow Sam and walk in the holes left by Sam's boots.

The day was beginning as he'd hoped. A beautiful sunrise, a stop at his favorite coffee shop to grab a cup of Java to go, and a predetermined visit to an ice fishing camp on the banks of the Connecticut River. First stop would be at the Connecticut/Massachusetts border.

Sam sipped his coffee and drove his Car 6 Blazer along Highway 5 heading North toward Massachusetts. He took a left side road that led him to a forested area bordered on the west by the Connecticut River and on the north by the Massachusetts state line. Presently a small parking lot appeared nestled inside a cove of evergreens. He pulled the mic from its holder on the cruiser's dashboard and keyed the mic. "419, State Park North by the river. I'll be 44 in five minutes." Sam was notifying Thompson Dispatch he had arrived at his location and would be out of the cruiser and on foot in five minutes.

"Roger, 419," came the reply.

Sam cracked open his cruiser door and stepped out onto packed snow. There had been enough vehicle activity to compact the snow in the tiny parking lot. Four pick-up trucks stood vigil in a far corner of the little parking lot awaiting the return of their owners. *Looks like they started early this morning,* he thought. *Got to give 'em credit, coming out this early on such a cold morning when they could be home sleeping or eating a hot breakfast.* Sam walked around the back of his truck and looked down the path that led to the river. It appeared as if the ice fisherman had already packed it down with their snowshoes. There were signs of a flat bottom equipment sled that was being hauled along also. *Won't need the snowshoes this time. The path goes right down to the lagoon and they'll have whatever snow is left on the ice shoveled off.* Traveller sat obediently in the front seat awaiting Sam's Command. Sam opened the Blazer's hatchback, "Come on, Trav." Traveller jumped across the front seats and into the fresh snow and trotted up to Sam's side.

The machine-packed snow path from the parking area was easy walking but hadn't frozen yet. Sam knew by afternoon it would be frozen and he'd have to walk alongside it. He felt the outside of his parka's left hip pocket to make sure he had brought his crampons along. After a little searching he confirmed their presence. Even if the path never froze, he knew he'd need them on the river ice anyway. Ice fishermen usually cut two or three holes apiece and the camp he intended to visit usually sported four to five anglers. That meant at least ten holes with baited tip ups that required checking. Fisheries and Game regulations required all tip ups be personally attended at all times. The angler's name was also required to be on or attached to the associated tip up. After the usual greetings and small talk, Sam was going to have to visit each tip up to ensure the rules were being followed. Good traction would be imperative especially if the wind was heavy or gusting.

As Sam and Traveller walked along the path he reveled in the picturesque surroundings around him. The snow hung from the pines as if it was dripping from the evergreen's branches. They appeared as upside down ice cream cones that had been skewered by an evergreen branch. The whole tree seemed to droop under the weight of the new fallen snow and provided a different kind of silence. It was the result of the snow-covered trees that insulated the forest from all of the sounds around him as well as those from far off. The air seemed fresher and cleaner enhanced by the pungent scent of pine, and as the sun rose above the tree tops, the white evergreen branches twinkled in the cold air. The only sound he heard was that of his boots as they swished through the light powder or crunched the newly packed snow.

They continued down the path to an intersection of four trails. To his right was a small clearing. He stopped for a moment to look around. It was empty but not lonely. The brilliance of colors mixed with the new snow and the dawning of a new day gave everything a fresh and lively look. Sam smiled. He felt privileged to be witnessing such natural beauty and wondered how many people would never be privy to a scene as special as the one before him

Presently the path began to climb a slight hill and then dropped into a small gulley, only to rise again to a small ridge line. Sam could see the river through the tree tops and knew it was time to veer left onto a snow-covered path that wound between the skeletons of charred trees, the result of a long past forest fire. After a five-minute walk along the ridge, an old elm tree stood sentry by the side of the path. It was the marker for the next trail that would take him and Traveller down to the river's icy bank. He turned and looked behind. Traveller obediently followed close behind.

Sam began his descent toward the river. As he approached, he began to hear the distant, muffled sounds of human voices. He stopped for a moment and reached into the right breast pocket of his uniform parka and pulled out a small pair of binoculars. He sighted on the river and focused out the trees. Sure enough, the ice fishermen were there. They scurried about, from hole to hole, tending to their tip ups, drilling holes, and tending the campfire. He counted four men and twenty-four ice holes with tip ups. Sam brought the binoculars down to his chest for a moment. *Hmm…Okay looks legal. Each man is allowed six tip ups but two of the guys are missing. Must be going to cut a few more holes when they show up.*

Just as Sam brought the glasses back up to his eyes, a fifth man came out onto the ice. *Okay, there we go. There's the fifth of the regulars. Still one missing. Guess they're not done cutting ice holes.*

Sam finally reached the end of the trail and stepped out onto the ice. The aroma of coffee perking over an open fire filled the air. He paused a moment to take in the surroundings. Traveller stood right next to him looking up waiting for Sam's next move. "Traveller, sit!" Sam knelt down and patted his dog on the head. "Stay here and watch me. I'll be back." Traveller sat on the packed snow and wagged his tail. Sam gave him a small dog treat and started for the campfire on the open ice. The anglers saw him the moment he emerged from the tree line and waved. Sam walked up to the first log that lay on the ice near the campfire and pulled out his crampons and sat down to put them on.

Everyone on the ice came over to meet him. Bill Lindsay was the first to say something. "Hey Warden, what's the matter…don't trust us? How about a coffee first?"

Sam looked up and smiled. Lindsay was a big man, about six feet two inches tall and two hundred and fifty pounds. He sported a beard and mustache and wore a red flannel shirt that covered a belly that hung over his belt. "You know me, Bill. I have to check the tip ups first and then we'll have some coffee."

The rest of the anglers had now joined Sam and Lindsay. Joe Sarkin shook his head from side to side. "Same old Sam… Mr. Boy Scout. How many years have you known us?"

Sam finished with the first crampon and was putting on the second. Without looking up, Sam replied, "How ya' doing, Joe? Known you twenty years and the rules haven't changed."

Sam stood up from the log. "You guys want to go check on your tip ups one last time before I make the rounds?"

A third angler spoke up rather sarcastically. It was Mike Sarkin, Joe's brother. "What're you gonna' do, Mr. Ranger, if we did do something wrong?"

Sam started for the tip ups, stopped in front of Mike and looked into his eyes. "I'll give you a ticket."

The five men watched as Sam went around to each tip up. Finally, Sam finished checking the last tip up and came back to the group as they stood on the ice. The sun had risen high in the sky creating a brilliance on the ice that would have been blinding had they not been wearing sunglasses. "Okay, guys,…now let me see your fishing licenses." Each man reached into their pockets and produced Connecticut fishing licenses. Sam nodded his head and looked at the group. "Okay, good deal. Now it's coffee time."

Joe Sarkin shook his head. "Just like that? You pull the game warden routine on us and now we're friends again?"

Bill Lindsay turned to Joe, "Knock it off, Joe. You're gonna' piss him off and ruin the whole day."

Sam showed no emotion. When no one spoke, he offered, "If you guys want to be alone, I'll be on my way."

Bill stepped in and grabbed Sam by the back of his shoulder. "He's just busting your ass, Sam. Come on… we got some kilbosa goin' too. We know you like it…got enough for your dog over there too."

The other four anglers followed behind Sam and Bill as they headed for the campfire. Sam smiled to himself as they walked. He realized the guys were just giving him a hard time because he knew them but that is precisely the reason he checked them.

Sam and the five ice anglers stood around the campfire sipping hot coffee. Steam rose from each of their mugs as they drank. There was an uneasy silence for the first couple of minutes then Joe Sarkin looked at Bill Lindsay. "Well, are you gonna' tell him or is it gonna' be one of us?"

Lindsay scowled at Joe a moment, and Sam looked up from his mug of coffee. "Tell me what," and directed his gaze at Sarkin.

Lindsay looked at Sam and answered. "The word is out that Jake Farmer has been trying to make a deal in prison with the parole board." Sam said nothing and looked back down into his mug of coffee. Sam was aware of the situation but said nothing.

Joe Sarkin asked, "How long's he been in now? Seems like a while."

Sam answered without looking up from his coffee. "He's been in a little over a year…of a two-year sentence."

Joe responded immediately, "Do you think they 'll cut him loose early? After all, he did spend almost a year in the hospital because of that brawl in the field with you." Joe was referring to a night up in New Hampshire two years ago when Sam and his group of wardens ambushed Jake Farmer's poaching ring.

Sam looked up and right at Joe. Joe continued, "A man that age wrestling a younger man like you and in the midst of being surrounded by a bunch of other game wardens... what was he thinking?"

Sam stared at Joe for a minute and the atmosphere grew more tense. Finally, Sam said, "You seem to know a lot about Jake Farmer's business, Joe." Sam kept his eyes set on Joe.

"Oh, now wait a minute," Joe was beginning to get defensive. "I was just wondering if you had heard." Joe paused. "The rumor is that he's coming after you when he gets out." Sam smiled and threw the remains of what coffee was still in his mug on the ice. He put the mug down on a log by the campfire.

Sam looked back at Joe, "Sounds like a lot of speculation to me. I know Farmer has to be pretty pissed but he hasn't had many visitors...in the hospital or in prison." Sam continued his eye lock with Joe.

Bill Lindsay broke the awkwardness. "Alright, alright. Are we out here to be gossiping or are we here to fish? We've got more holes to drill and fish to catch...come on you guys."

Sam picked up the auger lying next to his foot. "I'll drill a couple for you." He broke his eye lock with Joe, picked up the auger and walked to an open space in the ice to start drilling.

As Sam walked away, Bill Lindsay glared at Joe Sarkin, "What are you doing? The man came out here to spend some time with us and make sure we're all legal and you try to piss him off."

Sarkin shook his head. "Yeah well, we've known Sam a while but when it comes right down to it, he's still a fish cop and he'd pinch any one of us if he caught us doin' something illegal."

Lindsay grabbed Sarkin by the arm and turned him so the two men were facing each other. "Look, Sam is a warden…but he's a fair man too. Never seen him to not give the benefit of the doubt." Sarkin looked away to the river's bank. Bill continued, "C'mon, Joe. Go check some of your tip ups. Everything will be okay." Sarkin never looked up. He walked toward his gear bag and started to fiddle with some of his fishing rigs.

Sam had chosen a place in the middle of the frozen lagoon to drill an ice hole. It was about twenty feet from the closest hole and just far enough away where he could hear himself think. He turned the big auger into the ice and couldn't help but wonder why Joe Sarkin had any interest in Jake Farmer and where was he getting his information. He considered the fact that a lot of information gets leaked by individuals at the P.D and that was most likely where Joe had heard about Farmer. Someone goes home from work and tells a family member, then that person tells someone else, and so on. Sam also knew that each time a story is told it gets changed a little too, until very little of the original story remains.

Suddenly Sam's radio crackled to life. "Headquarters to 419."

Sam unclipped his portable radio from his duty belt and keyed the mic. "419, Connecticut River North, on the ice."

Dispatch replied, "Roger 419. We have a possible sick raccoon harassing some citizens on the east side of town. We'll give you details as you get enroute."

Sam acknowledged the call, "Roger, on my way."

Sam put down the ice auger and walked past the group of ice anglers who had by now settled into a work regimen, tending their tips ups, baiting hooks and stoking the fire. They all waved as Sam made for the tree line. He decided to keep his crampons on until he got back to the Blazer as the packed snow he walked in on was probably frozen by now.

Sam glanced over at the edge of the frozen lagoon. Traveller sat in the same spot staring at Sam as he approached. The dog wagged his tail but remained seated. When Sam cleared the ice he knelt down in the snow and called Traveller. "Come here, boy." Traveller ran up to Sam and nuzzled his head into Sam's chest and shoulder. Sam produced another treat. "Good dog, good boy." Sam rubbed Traveller vigorously around his head, shoulders and back. "Okay, let's head back to the cruiser." Sam stood and started away from the lagoon and Traveller followed dutifully in his tracks.

As the pair approached the trail that led to the ridge, Sam decided to take a short cut. It was barely a path and little more than a cut line (a roughly cut path) through the forest but it would get him to the main trail a lot sooner. Sam took the cut line and headed north. He stopped as he saw another person approaching him. It was surprising to see anyone on this trail since it wasn't well defined or travelled and it was harder walking because of the newly fallen snow.

Sam remained where he was and waited for the hiker. It turned out to be one of the missing ice fishermen. "Hey, Jimmy. What are you doing on this trail?"

Jimmy seemed a little nervous and in a hurry. At first, it didn't look like he was going to stop. "Uh, hey Sam. Just taking a short cut to the lagoon. Are the boys down there?"

Sam didn't move from his place but continued to watch the man. "Yeah, they're there, Jim. What's the rush?"

Jimmy's eyes darted all around the forest. "No rush, no rush. Just looking to get to the tip ups…you know."

Sam looked at the large back pack Jimmy had strapped to his back. "What in hell are you carrying, Jim? Staying a week or what?"

Jimmy still had not met Sam's eyes. "Oh, the boys are hungry. I got a lot of food to cook."

Sam stepped to the side of the trail to let him pass. "Okay, have a good day." Sam watched the man walk swiftly toward the lagoon, occasionally stumbling in the deep snow. *Something isn't right here,* he thought. Sam turned and continued down the trail already marked by Jimmy's boot prints.

Five minutes down the trail Sam noticed a lot of prints in the snow all confined to a small area. Traveller ran up ahead and began sniffing around at what appeared to be a grain pile. It had been freshly staged. Sam looked at the surrounding trees and saw fresh cuts on them as if someone had cut a corridor to the carefully placed pile of food. At the end of the cut line was a tree stand, complete with a metal ladder that rose steeply to its platform.

Sam looked at Traveller. "Could this be the tree stand we've been looking for?" There were no markings or identification on the apparatus. Traveller wagged his tail back at Sam and sat in the snow. "Stay here, boy. I'm going to get up in that stand to see what the hunter sees." Rung by rung, Sam climbed the ladder and spun around at the top to place himself in a sitting position on the stand's platform. There were actually three grain piles and a salt lick, at the end of three separate corridors, all freshly cut to remove tree branches from the line of site, or trajectory to the bait. Sam sat and studied the area. Adjacent to the grain piles were night vision cameras strapped to three separate trees. The entire site was illegal and set up to entrap a hungry or curious deer. It was a poaching site for sure.

Sam spoke aloud but under his breath, "Son of bitch! Assholes!" He looked down at Traveller who sat at the ladder's base wagging his tail. The tail's back and forth movement caused a fanlike shape to appear in the fresh snow. Sam looked around his position in the tree stand. More branches had been cut close to the tree trunks that might cause conflict with any kind of movement on the stand's platform. Sam began to think the situation out in his mind. *This guy is an archer. There is just enough room to pull back an arrow in three directions. The shavings on the ground match the cuts on the trees that are trimmed in the corridors. He lures the deer in by baiting them and has the night vision cameras timed to come on after dark. He can see how big the animals are and what time they're coming in to get the bait.*

He sat there thinking for a moment. *Wait a minute. Jimmy just came down this path and his boot prints are the only prints in the snow. All that eye action and nervousness I saw. He probably came to refill the grain piles and change out the night vision film. I bet this is his stand…the bastard. Ice fishing my ass!*

Sam pulled out his portable radio and keyed the mic. He was going to need officer back up. "419…State Park North by the river."

Dispatch came back. "419, go."

"I've run into a scenario on my way out of the woods. I'm going to need a ten."

"Roger, 419. Are you okay?"

Sam keyed his mic. "Affirmative. Have a possible situation at the lagoon. So far all is quiet."

"Roger, 419." There was a short pause then Dispatch continued, "419, wait one. The LT wants a word." After a few moments, Dispatch came back on the air. "419, hold your position. 402 will be your ten. Previous call is cancelled. Orders are to meet him on the ridge, east of your position."

Sam kept his finger off the radio's key and spoke aloud. "402? Why is Lieutenant Alban coming out here?" Sam keyed the mic, "419, Roger. Will meet 402 on the ridge and intersection of the park's main trail." Dispatch copied and signed off. Sam shrugged his shoulders and looked at Traveller. "C'mon, Trav. Let's go meet Alban. He wants to come play with us." Traveller stood and followed Sam up the trail to the ridge.

About thirty minutes passed and Sam saw a dark figure against the snow working its way down the main trail into the gulley. He pulled the binoculars from his parka and focused in on the moving shape. It was Alban. Sam was relieved. Not being able to leave the area meant not moving around too much and the cold was beginning to take its toll. Sam reached down and rubbed Traveller's entire body to warm him up a little, and gave him another dog treat. He looked at his watch. It was almost ten AM. Sam reached down and massaged each one of Traveller's paws. He removed a glove from one hand and held it against each of Traveller's paw pads to warm them.

Finally, Alban arrived. "So, you finally decided to call for back up."

Sam replied, "Didn't mean for you to come out, LT. It's colder than hell out here!"

Alban waved off the comment with a flip of his hand. "Ah, that's okay. I was doing this stuff when you were still in high school, Sam. Kinda' miss it. Besides, the entire shift is on snow patrol or out sick with the flu. You gave me an opportunity." Alban had been looking out over the ridge toward the ice-covered lagoon as he spoke and turned toward Sam. "So, what have we got?"

Sam explained the tree stand with its grain piles and night vision cameras. Alban said nothing as he listened.

Sam mentioned the uneasy atmosphere on the ice with the fishermen and the sudden appearance of Jimmy on one of the less used trails. Alban thought for a moment. "We've had reports of a tree stand down here somewhere that was not part of the lottery. Looks like you and Traveller finally found it. Show me."

The two wardens and Traveller walked back down the ridge to the illegal stand. After a quick inspection Alban stood in the snow and nodded his head. "Yup, smells bad. I think we have something here." Alban looked to the ice fisherman out on the lagoon and nodded in their direction. "And I think they're part of it too."

Sam nodded back at Alban. "How do you want to handle it?" Alban was looking out toward the lagoon. "If it is them, and this is," Alban paused, "that guy Jimmy's tree stand, we have to catch them in the act. You didn't see him check the cameras or bait the grain piles so we're going to have to come back…at night." He looked at Sam. "Tonight."

— — —

Sam and Lieutenant Alban knelt in the night snow on the ridge overlooking the lagoon. They had returned to the police station for the rest of the morning to warm up and plan a sting on the would-be poachers. Now, they were back on the ridge just above the suspect tree stand. Sam looked out to the frozen lagoon and saw a fire burning on the ice. The smallest light or fire is easily noticeable on a dark night even at great distances. "They still have a fire going. These guys are hard core."

Alban could see the same fire and asked, "Can you make out how many of them are out there?"

Sam pulled out his night vision binoculars and raised them to his eyes. He focused out the tree limbs and got a pretty clear picture of the crew on the ice. "Looks like they're all still there…all the same people."

Alban looked at his watch – eight PM. Alban rubbed his gloved hands together. "They probably went home after we left to warm up and came back out after sunset…too cold to have been here all day."

Sam nodded his head in affirmance as he watched the group through his binoculars. "Yeah, I noticed quite a few more tracks in the snow…going and coming, when we came back out tonight. I think they were planning the whole thing. That's why they were so skittish out on the ice this morning."

Alban slowly stood up from the snow but stayed in a crouch. "Okay, Sam. Let's start working our way down off this ridge. Less likely for them to see our silhouettes against the night sky." Obediently, Sam followed as Alban worked his way down the wooded slope. They ignored the trail as they knew anyone coming into the area would probably be using the easiest way to travel and that would also be the area the would-be poachers would be watching. Alban stopped by an area where there was a lot of deadfall. It was about thirty feet west of the tree stand. The tangled debris of several trees and broken branches would be enough to camouflage their dark body shapes against the white snow in the forest.

Sam knelt down beside Alban as the pair continued to watch the party on the ice. Sam pushed the indiglo button on his watch. It was nine PM. Alban spoke first. "Let's hope they start to move soon. It feels like the temperature is starting to drop again." Sam nodded his head in affirmance as he watched through his night vision binoculars. The men on the ice sat by the fire drinking something. They were probably pouring brandy into their coffee mugs for added warmth. Faint but muffled voices travelled across the frozen lagoon and were muffled even more as the human sounds tried to penetrate the forest.

Finally, one of the men began to rifle through his back pack. It was Jimmy. Another stood from his seat on the ice and walked over to the equipment sled that sat motionless on the frozen lagoon. He untied the ropes that stretched across the sled's girth and pulled back the blanket. It was Joe Sarkin. Joe reached down and lifted a compound bow from the top of the sled.

"Okay, here we go," Sam whispered to Alban. "Sarkin is pulling a bow from that sled out there." Sam continued to watch, "…and now he's clipping some arrows to the side of it."

Alban watched the group as Sam narrated the action on the ice. "Okay, game on. Sit quiet and we'll let them come to us. Does anyone have rifles or handguns?"

Sam was focusing the binoculars. "Nope. They're all beginning to stand now but I can't see what they might have attached to their belts or under their coats. I'm sure at least one of them has a handgun and they probably all have knives, so be advised, six of them and two of us."

Alban was still watching the soon to be poaching party. "Roger that. Stay calm and let 'em come."

The six men walked to the lagoon's frozen edge. They stopped and were talking quietly for a few minutes. Joe Sarkin handed the bow over to Jimmy and Jimmy checked his watch again. There was some kind of group agreement and then Jimmy headed into the woods by himself. The others turned and walked back toward the campfire.

Alban knelt down a little lower in the snow. "Okay Sam, it's time to rock and roll. He's heading right for us. We have to wait 'till he gets into the stand. After he gets situated I'll make the announcement and you get ready to go after the guys on the ice."

Sam kept his eyes on the approaching Jimmy. "Got it, LT."

Jimmy approached the tree stand using the same path as Sam had used earlier in the day. He cut left off the main trail and was headed right for the tree stand. Alban murmured to Sam, "Okay, go." Sam rose silently, and in a crouch circled around to the right of Jimmy. He made a wide arc so as to stay out of earshot. The plan was to have Sam in position near the lagoon's edge but between the guys on the ice and Alban. When Sam was in position he clicked his radio mic twice to signal Alban he was ready.

Jimmy stood at the base of his tree stand and looked up to its platform. It was about twenty feet off the ground. Jimmy slung his bow over his right shoulder and began to climb the stand's ladder. Several times his boots slipped on the icy rungs but he managed to stay on the ladder. Once he arrived at the platform, he turned as Sam had earlier, to get himself into a seated position. The darkness of night helped to hide any marks in the snow from Sam's visitation earlier in the day.

Jimmy sat quietly atop the tree stand and checked his watch. *Almost time for that big doe*, he thought. He pulled an arrow from the side of the bow and knocked it loosely on the bow's drawstring and handle. Twenty minutes passed. Jimmy was freezing. He held the bow between his thighs and tried to rub his gloved hands together. Suddenly there was the sound of a snapping stick. Jimmy stayed perfectly still. There was another snap and then a scrape of something against a tree. The doe was approaching slowly and cautiously.

Slowly, Jimmy craned his neck to the left and saw the big doe approaching him from the ten o'clock position. She came up to the salt lick and sniffed. A few moments passed and she raised her head and looked about the area. Alban was down wind of her in the deadfall and just to the right of the tree stand. The doe began to get comfortable and walked up to the grain pile straight out in front of Jimmy. She was now about forty feet from the tree stand. She raised her head one more time and sniffed the air. There were no signs of danger, no indications of any other creatures. She lowered her head and nibbled at the grain pile...cautiously at first. The doe lifted her head again, paused, and quickly lowered it again and began eating.

Jimmy slowly brought the bow out in front of him and began to draw the arrow back. His fingers and arms were a little stiff from waiting in the cold. Just as he brought the arrow back to the shooting position, the compound bow relaxed so he could steady his aim. Alban rose from the tangle of deadfall and shouted. "Hold it! Don't move!" Connecticut state law required that for a bow hunter to actually be considered "hunting," the arrow must first be knocked. Being knocked in the bowstring was akin to be loaded and ready to shoot.

Alban's surprise announcement almost caused Jimmy to drop the bow. The doe looked up suddenly and bounded into the darkness without a sound. Alban stood behind the tangle of deadfall with his revolver raised and trained on Jimmy. "Thompson Fish and Game. Relax that arrow, then let the bow fall to the ground. Arrow first." Jimmy looked straight ahead into the darkness. He could hear the voice from below but couldn't tell exactly where it was coming from. Alban coaxed Jimmy, "Let the arrow fall son. Nice and easy…let it drop." Jimmy obeyed. "Now the bow." The bow fell into the powdery snow almost without a sound. Alban lowered his gun but kept it drawn. "Good boy. Now call in your buddies. Tell 'em you need some help."

Sam watched as Alban controlled the situation at the tree stand. Then he heard Jimmy shout, "Hey guys! I need a hand out here." Sam was in a deep crouch in the snow just off the main trail but near the lagoon's edge. He turned to see if there was a reaction from the guys on the ice. Obviously, they heard Jimmy's call. Their heads all turned in the direction of the call. If it had been daytime, Sam would be in plain sight. He kept low and remained motionless.

Bill Lindsay was the first to stand from his camp chair by the fire. "Was that Jimmy calling for us?" Joe and Mike Sarkin remained seated but still looked in the direction of the call. Joe reached down and felt for his boot knife on his right leg. Mike reached inside his parka and felt for his.380 semi-automatic that rested in a shoulder holster under his left arm.

Joe stood and answered Bill without looking at him. "Yeah, that was Jimmy all right."

Now, Mike stood up, "Let's go see what he wants."

Bill started for the lagoon's edge but Joe stopped him. "Wait. All of us? Maybe one of us should stay by the fire."

Bill stopped and smirked at Joe. "He said, 'Guys, I need some help.' Maybe he fell out of the tree stand."

Joe was skeptical. "I don't know…feels funny."

Bill turned and headed for the trail head. "I'm going… Mike you coming?" Mike looked at Joe and back at the other two fishermen who remained seated. He took his hand out of his parka and followed Bill to the trailhead at the edge of the lagoon. Joe shook his head in disgust and followed.

"Call us if you need us," one of the larger ice fishermen shouted from his comfortable place by the fire, and threw another log on. He raised his beer as if in salute to their departing backsides and sipped on his beer.

As the group approached, Sam pressed himself against the base of a large swamp elm. They seemed to be walking right toward him and changed direction as they left the ice and stepped onto the snow packed trail. One by one, each man walked by Sam, their attention focused in the direction of the tree stand.

"Who are you?" Jimmy sat bolt upright in the tree stand, looking straight ahead into the darkness.

Alban remained behind the tangle of deadfall. "Lieutenant Alban, Thompson Fish and Game. You're under arrest for luring deer and hunting after sunset." Jimmy started to say something but Alban cut him off. "Be quiet and stay where you are until your buddies get here. When they see you, tell 'em you dropped your bow and your legs are cramped from the cold." Alban paused and added, "I'm not alone and we have you surrounded so if you say anything it'll only go worse for you. Do you understand?"

Jimmy's throat began to tighten up. "Yes, sir."

Sam watched the backs of the so-called ice fisherman as they faded into the dark forest. *Okay, two still on the ice, three on foot in the woods and one in a tree stand. If we get the four in the woods, the other two are going to book. That's okay because their buddies will give up their names anyhow.* Sam waited until they were out of ear shot before he started following. He stayed just far enough behind to keep the parka of the last man in sight.

Alban watched the three men from the ice approach the tree stand. They began to shout his name into the night air.

Alban looked up at Jimmy, "Okay, son. Let 'em know where you are. Say, 'over here' so they know you're still around."

Jimmy looked up into the night air, "Over here. I'm still in the stand."

Bill Lindsay, and the two Sarkin brothers stepped off the path and into the cleared area below the tree stand. Bill looked up at the frozen Jimmy. "What's the matter, Jim? We heard your call." Jimmy said nothing. He continued to stare out into the darkness. It was a feeble attempt to alert his comrades that something was wrong. Bill looked at Joe Sarkin. "What's wrong with him? Looks frozen solid."

Joe looked around the cleared area. "Something's not right."

Jimmy remembered Alban's threat. "Guys, I dropped my bow. It's somewhere down there. Can't get down the ladder…legs are all cramped up." Joe took a step back from the tree stand and scanned the entire area.

Alban noticed Joe's attention and took the opportunity. He stepped from behind the pile of deadfall. "Fish and Game. Keep your hands where I can see 'em." Alban had his.357 Smith and Wesson revolver leveled at the three men as they stood in the snow. They were taken completely by surprise and were still trying to digest the ambush.

Joe Sarkin reacted immediately. "Fuck! I told you assholes." Joe Sarkin kicked at the snow and turned away from Alban. Mike Sarkin reached inside his parka for the.380 semi-automatic pistol under his arm.

Alban saw the move and focused on Mike. "Hold it. Hands in the air! Slowly remove your hand from your coat."

Joe Sarkin wheeled around knowing Alban was distracted by Mike, and reached down for his boot knife. In one graceful move, Joe pulled the knife from its sheath and threw it at Alban. The knife sailed through the night air and stuck hard into a tree just behind Alban. It missed his right ear by inches.

Alban heard the knife cut the air as it passed and penetrated the tree behind him. The blade made a thudding sound as it vibrated in the hard wood. Jimmy remained in the tree stand and watched in horror as the scene unfolded below him. Alban swung his revolver to his right and shot low. The.357 hollow point struck Joe at mid-thigh causing him to spin around backwards and fall into the snow screaming in pain. The bullet had hit his thigh bone and shattered it. Alban remained calm and brought his gun back to Mike. Mike was pulling the.380 out of his parka when another shot came from behind. It was the thundering sound of another.357 revolver behind him. The unexpected blast caused Mike to hesitate. "Drop it Mike." Sam stood ten feet behind the two men left standing. He had fired into the air over Mike's head.

Alban stood facing the men, gun still leveled at the two perpetrators. "Party's over boys. You are covered front and back. Next man that makes a move is dead. Mike let your weapon fall to the snow."

Bill Lindsay realized the worst was over and took the opportunity. "Look officers, I knew about the tree stand but didn't know they were using it." He paused a moment as he read Alban's facial expression. "I'm not part of this…really. I knew they had cameras but I didn't care, much less know what they were doing with them."

Alban looked at the man disapprovingly. "Save it for the judge, pal. All I know is that you're out here with them, so as far as I know, you're part of it."

Alban looked over at Sam. "Where's the other two, Sergeant?" Alban addressed Sam by his rank since officers were trained not to use given names in front of the suspect parties.

Sam pointed toward the ice. "Looks like they're leaving." Alban glanced down toward the lagoon. Moonlight reflected off the dark ice like a spotlight and showed an abandoned campfire and two dark figures desperately trying to flee the area as they slipped and tumbled on the lagoon's glare ice.

Alban smiled, "We'll catch up with them later."

Sam nodded at the writhing figure in the snow. Blood spattered the entire area. Joe's screaming and complaining was subsiding revealing an indication that shock was beginning to set in. "I'll check him for any more weapons if you can call for an airlift."

Alban nodded in an affirmative way and pulled his portable radio from his belt. "402 to Headquarters."

Dispatch had been waiting for the call, "402, go."

"Our position is State Park North by the river. Shots fired, one man down, three more in custody. Two heading south on the river ice from our position. Require a chopper ASAP. Victim has a gunshot wound to the right thigh and bleeding badly. Expedite!"

Dispatch replied, "Got it, 402. We need a location for the chopper's LZ (landing zone)."

Alban keyed his mic again, "Tell the chopper pilot to target east side of the river's lagoon area by the state border. Look for a clearing north of the main trail, one half mile east of the lagoon's eastern bank, between the two ridges. One of us will meet the chopper there. When we see it, one of us will signal with our mag lite."

"Roger 402. Be advised we have ground parties on the way. Need a well-being check on you and 419."

Alban replied, "400 units are good. 419 is with the injured party."

"Dispatch rogers that. Chopper is airborne, ETA is ten minutes."

Alban let out a breath and clipped his radio back to his belt. He looked up at the terrified Jimmy freezing in the tree stand. "Climb down out of there, son and stand next your buddies. Hands where I can see 'em."

Sam finished checking Joe Sarkin for weapons and discovered he was carrying a.38 special snub nose in his parka. He put a tourniquet on Joe's leg and looked at Alban. "Sarkin's secured, LT."

Alban glanced over at Sam, "Good. I'll stay here with these guys. You head up to the clearing to meet the chopper."

Sam stood up from the blood-soaked snow and said, "Okay LT." He took a last look at Joe Sarkin laying in the snow holding his leg and trudged off in the direction of the main trail.

The chopper was right on time and Sam arrived in the clearing just as the chopper was turning in from the river's edge. The pilot saw Sam's light in the dark clearing and turned on his 'Night Sun' spotlight positioned on the chopper's belly, lighting the entire clearing as if it were daytime. Sam shielded his eyes and stepped back to the clearing's edge as the pilot put his machine down in the white powder.

The EMTs jumped out with a stretcher and followed Sam to the tree stand. About the same time, two patrols of game wardens and town police were approaching the ridge above on foot.

A dark forest normally lonely and quiet, was lit up like Christmas time with spotlights and aircraft strobes, human activity and all the urgent voices that came with it. The EMTs strapped Joe to the stretcher and towed him to the waiting helicopter. Alban held his gun on Mike, Jimmy, and Bill Lindsay as the reserve game wardens handcuffed them. The police officers took pictures of the poaching site, collected evidence, and wrapped police caution tape around the entire area.

As they all headed for the waiting chopper, Alban gave the game wardens instructions to take Jimmy, Bill and Mike out on foot and he'd meet up with them at the P.D. Everyone paused when they arrived at the clearing and watched the EMTs load Joe Sarkin into the chopper. Alban looked at Sam. "It's been a long day, Sam. Good pinch though."

Sam watched the chopper as the door closed and the rotors started to wind up. "I bet you'll think twice about coming out to be my back up again."

Alban turned and looked Sam in the face. "I'd do it again in a heartbeat." He put his hand up to give Sam a high five and Sam slapped it with his gloved hand. The two officers turned and followed the ground patrols with their prisoners up the next ridge to the waiting cruisers.

The chopper was airborne and heading for the hospital. As it disappeared into the cold, dark night, the signature sound of its rotor blades dissipated as if enveloped by the blackness, and when the back of the last man's parka disappeared over the gulley's east ridge, the little clearing became a dark and quiet place once again. Man had left the area.

★★★★

CHAPTER 14

Joe Sarkin's thigh bone had been shattered so badly the rescue chopper was advised that Hilltown was the best choice for orthopedic surgeries of such magnitude. The chopper pilot concurred and deposited him at Hilltown General Hospital one hundred miles northeast of Thompson.

Police Lieutenant Dan Murdock stood outside Joe Sarkin's hospital room. Murdock had been called in the morning after Alban and Sam had arrested the group of deer poachers by the lagoon and assigned the task of questioning him on the two runaway ice anglers and information about the rumor regarding Jake Farmer's revenge on Sam Moody.

Murdock stood patiently outside Sarkin's room waiting for the doctor to grant him time to see the patient. Eventually, the door opened and a doctor in a white lab coat came out, gave Murdock a glance and without breaking stride said, "Okay you have fifteen minutes. He's in a lot of pain and I just sedated him again." The doctor stopped, turned and looked at the lieutenant. "Do you cops have to carry such big guns? That .357 hollow point shattered the entire middle section of his thigh bone. We're going to have to put a metal rod in there for sure." Murdock looked at the doctor stoically and said nothing. The doctor shook his head in disgust and walked away. "Only fifteen minutes…if you can get that much from him."

Murdock walked in and sat down in a guest chair near the foot of the bed. Sarkin's eyes were closed but he opened them slowly when he heard someone sit down in the chair. Sarkin frowned. "Who are you? Can't be a doctor...not wearin' one of those white gowns."

Murdock replied, "I'm Lieutenant Dan Murdock... attached to the Connecticut State Police. I just want to ask a few questions about some of the people you were with the other night when you were...injured."

Sarkin's face turned into a snarl. "You mean when that bastard game warden shot me!"

Murdock quickly added, "Well, you threw a hunting knife at him, Joe."

Sarkin became sarcastic, "Oh, big tough game warden. So, he shoots me when all I had was a knife."

Murdock leaned forward in his chair. "Let me remind you, Joe. He could have killed you." Murdock paused and raised an eyebrow, "It would be in your best interest to start telling the truth ...right now." Murdock paused then continued, "You were carrying a .38 special snubnose in your coat pocket, Joe. So, let me see," Murdock stood from the chair and looked toward the ceiling. "Assaulting a uniformed officer, intent to kill, poaching...I'd say you had better start cooperating right now and drop that fucking attitude or you're going away for a long time." Murdock looked down at the prostrate Sarkin and shouted, "Do you understand me you fucking loser? You're going away for a long time, so you better come clean. I'll walk out that door right now and put a report together based only on what you've shown me so far, and leave you to the prosecutors. They're like wolves, man, ...and when they find out you tried to kill a warden... shit! They'll eat you alive. The DA would just love to have his day with you in court."

Sarkin was wide awake now and tried to lean forward from his pillow. "I hate you fucking cops, especially those wardens."

Murdock smiled and walked around the bed and looked down at Sarkin. He knew he was getting to him. "Yeah, well, we hate you more."

Murdock decided to let Sarkin stew for awhile. Sarkin sat with the back of his bed slightly elevated and his arms folded across his chest. Murdock reached into his coat and pulled out a business card. "This is my card, Joe. My phone number is on it and I hope you decide to call me…for your sake." He placed the card on the portable tray table in front of Sarkin. "I want to know who the two guys on the ice were." Sarkin said nothing but continued to look straight ahead. Murdock continued, "You know…the ones you left behind while you, Lindsay and your brother went to check on Jimmy. Also, you mentioned you heard Jake Farmer is coming after Sam Moody when he gets out of prison. I'd like to hear who told you that and where you heard it." Sarkin didn't acknowledge Murdock or anything he was saying. He just sat there in his hospital bed, as if he was alone in the room.

Murdock walked back to the chair he had been sitting in and picked up his file folder. It was obvious Sarkin was done talking for today. Before he left the room, Murdock turned back to Sarkin. "Think about what I said Joe. You've got nothing to lose…except your freedom." Murdock turned and left Sarkin alone in the room.

★★★★

CHAPTER 15

I t was a bright sunny day in early March and State's lawyer Thomas Dooley was driving out to the state penitentiary to visit his client, Jake Farmer. Dooley was in deep thought as he drove down Highway 19 in southern Connecticut. The scenery passed but he never saw it. Part of him felt guilty for his stance on defending whatever Farmer's rights were after all he had done, and another part felt as if he was just doing his job as a state defense lawyer. He satisfied himself with the belief that he was only performing a service for the state and that had no bearing on his personal feeling about the crime that had been committed.

Jake had now been incarcerated for ten months not including his six and a half months in the hospital after the firefight in New Hampshire. He had been writing letters and hounding Dooley with phone calls when he could make them. Visitations with Jake were getting more and more tension filled as Jake wanted to see progress with his plea for early parole. Dooley was beginning to dread his weekly scheduled meetings with the man. If he didn't tell Jake what he wanted to hear, Jake was all over him. The conversation always ended with Jake standing up from his assigned visitor's booth berating him and shouting obscenities. The guard would always end the session early and most of what

Dooley had intended to cover was either not discussed or incomplete.

The more Dooley thought about it, the more he questioned why he should keep the case. He realized Farmer was a bad seed and the situation was complicated about getting the parole board to understand that it was Farmer's altercation with Sam Moody that caused his time in the hospital and as that went, should be counted as time spent against his sentence.

Suddenly, Tom realized he was turning into the prison's long driveway. As his car approached the main gate a guard stepped out of a small guard house to wave him down. Dooley was getting nervous. He murmured aloud in the car, "Well, I'm here. I don't know how he's going to take this news but I'm obligated to present it." The guard checked Dooley's credentials and let him pass. *Here we go*, he thought.

Thomas Dooley, state assigned defense lawyer for Jake Farmer sat in a glass fronted booth in the prison's visitor center. He felt anxious and nervous at the same time. His stomach felt queasy and he was perspiring. What kind of wrath would Jake impose on him this time. Dooley could only hope the news he had for the former game warden turned poacher was acceptable.

The guard ushered Farmer to a seat across from Dooley. There was a bullet proof plate of glass that separated the two men. Farmer nodded at the phone that lay in front of Dooley. Reluctantly, Dooley picked it up but said nothing. Farmer stared into the lawyer's eyes and snarled, "Well, what have you got for me Dooley? And it better be good."

The guard intervened, "Hey, Jake. Watch your mouth and your temper or I'll walk you back to your cell right now. No more of those explosions. Understand?" Jake kept staring through the glass at Dooley. The guard repeated himself much louder. "Farmer, I asked you a question." The guard started toward Farmer while pulling his baton from its holster.

Jake, not taking his eyes off of his visitor answered, "Yeah, yeah, I heard you…I got it." The guard stopped and paused for a moment, nodded at Dooley behind the glass, and returned to his place by the door.

Dooley took a deep breath. "Good afternoon, Jake. I do have some news for you. I met with the parole board last week and they reviewed your plea for early parole."

Jake slammed his fist down on the countertop in front of him. "Well, get to it for Christ's sake."

The guard shouted, "Farmer!"

Jake held up his right hand with his fingers spread apart. "Okay, okay…sorry." He continued to stare down his lawyer.

Dooley began to speak slowly, "Well, they reviewed everything, Jake. They looked at your past service, interviewed people you knew, etcetera, and basically did their homework on you." Dooley took a deep breath and continued. "The board will consider a hearing for early parole on the condition you participate in an interview about some rumors that have been reported to the Thompson Police Department."

Farmer rolled his eyes while raising his hands in a questioning manner. Then he took a breath and exhaled trying to gather some composure. "Okay, what is it now? What rumor?"

Dooley braced himself. "The parole board knows who you have had for visitors…when…and how many times. Your outside phone calls were also monitored." Dooley paused and looked deep into Farmer's eyes, "Especially those to another prison. Some of these people have been talking about those visits…and you know…when a story gets repeated, especially more than once, it generally gets changed a little…sometimes a lot."

Immediately, Jake could feel his blood pressure begin to rise. He told himself to stay calm, stay in control. He remembered a phone call he had with his brother-in-law and former accomplice Billy Jaggs. *That fuckin' Jaggs. Must have said something.* He took another deep breath and exhaled audibly. "Okay, Dooley. I don't know what they're looking for but I'll grant the interview."

Dooley wrote some notes down and closed his notebook. "Okay, we're done then." Dooley smiled at Jake. "Just tell them the truth. Don't tell them what you think they want to hear, don't sugar coat it. Just give them the facts plain and simple….and above all, don't keep apologizing for what you think they think. They're looking for, no attitude, quick and simple answers…not excuses or apologies."

Jake began to relax a little and looked down at the countertop in front of him. He nodded his head to indicate he understood and asked. "When?"

Dooley stood up from the chair. "Next week - Wednesday afternoon."

Jake thought to himself, *Mid-March. I may be outta' here by May first.*

★★★★

CHAPTER 16

It had been three days since Lieutenant Dan Murdock had seen Joe Sarkin. He walked into the Thompson Police Department for a visit with Fish and Game Lieutenant Alban before he ventured further north to visit the injured poacher. Dan figured he had given Joe ample time to get things straightened out in his own mind and give some consideration about the ultimatum he had left him with. He hoped Sarkin had decided to play along and answer some questions about the missing ice anglers that fled the scene the night he was shot. Also, on the agenda was the rumor about Farmer getting revenge on Sam Moody when he gets released from prison and where that information came from. It was imperative Sarkin give out that information as Sam's life as well as his family's could be endangered.

Murdock walked down the long corridor and knocked at Alban's office door. There was a momentary pause followed by, "Come."

Murdock opened the door to see Alban busily sifting through a multitude of paperwork. He stopped just past the door, straightened up and announced himself, "Lieutenant Dan Murdock, Connecticut State Police."

Alban motioned Murdock in with a flip of his hand and without looking up said, "What can I do for you, Lieutenant?"

Murdock remained where was. "May I come in for a quick discussion about Joe Sarkin?"

At the mention of Sarkin's name, Alban looked up. "Oh, I'm sorry. I get so wound up in all this paperwork I sometimes forget my manners." Alban stood and motioned for Murdock to come forward and take a seat.

Once Murdock was seated Alban asked him again, "What can I do for you?"

Murdock sat bolt upright in the chair and stared right at Alban. "I'm going back to Hilltown General Hospital to visit with the man you shot in the woods last week."

Alban sat up in his chair. "Oh, I see, and you're assigned to interview me too?"

Murdock shifted in his seat. "No, that will be someone else. I just wanted to brief you on what I'm doing with the man you shot. I already had one visit with him and he didn't want to talk so I gave him an ultimatum."

Alban put a hand in the air. "Whoa, whoa. Let's go back a minute. You referred to Sarkin as the man I shot...twice. Do I detect an attitude here?"

Murdock didn't flinch. "No attitude, Lieutenant. You did shoot the man...correct?"

Alban's blood pressure began to rise. "Yes, I did...right in the leg. I could have taken him out because he had just thrown a hunting knife at my head, but I elected to disable him instead." It was only then that Alban realized the trooper was merely testing him to see if it was really self-defense. *What am I doing? This guy is just testing me as to why I really shot Sarkin. He's purposely trying to piss me off.*

Murdock remained stoic but let a little smile start. "I have to ask these questions, Lieutenant...make sure it was a legitimate shoot."

Alban leaned back in his chair. 'Yeah, I realize that. It's still a little soon for you to be playing with my head though. Do you think I'm happy about blowing a guy's leg apart? I just reacted and I admit I'm feeling a little sensitive about it."

Murdock nodded his head. "I got the response I was looking for. We don't want any cowboys out there and to hear you say you're feeling...a little sensitive about it, tells me what I wanted to know."

The two lieutenants stared at each other for a moment and Murdock continued. "Just an FYI, Sergeant Moody found a .38 special snubby tucked inside Sarkin's shoulder holster while you were holding the other three at bay. He removed it but didn't tell you about it as it looked as if you had your hands full already. Sarkin would have probably used that on you next had you not disabled him." Alban drew a sigh of relief. It appeared the investigator concurred with his actions against Sarkin.

Alban leaned forward onto his desk. "Okay Lieutenant, what's going on with Sarkin?" Murdock began, "He started to give me 'the big bad cop shot me' routine so I warned him that if he didn't come clean and tell us what we wanted to know he might be going away for a long time."

Alban nodded his head as he stared at his desk. Murdock continued, "I just wanted to let you know I was going back up to Hillside to get him to talk and that I have your boy... Sam's best interest in mind."

Alban looked up and said, "I appreciate that."

Murdock stood from his chair and reached out to shake Alban's hand. "Good to meet you. I'll send you a report of what Sarkin gives me."

Alban stood and shook Murdock's hand. "Thanks."

★★★★

CHAPTER 17

Dan Murdock walked up to Joe Sarkin's room. The Do Not Disturb card had been pushed aside and the door was cracked partly open. Murdock stopped in front of the door and gently knocked three times. At first there was no answer. Murdock raised his hand to knock again and an irritated reply came from within. "Yeah, come in."

Murdock pushed open the bedroom door to find Joe Sarkin sitting up in bed, cleaned up and shaven. Even his hair had been combed. Sarkin stared blankly at Murdock in the doorway. He knew why the trooper was back and was prepared. An awkward silence followed and Murdock was first to speak. "Well, good morning, Sunshine. Looks like you got all prettied up for me."

Sarkin's blank stare turned into a sneer. "Cut the shit, Murdock." Don't make this any harder than it's got to be. I'm gonna' talk but don't push me."

Murdock came forward and sat in the guest chair by the foot of the bed. "Okay, Joe. Let's get right to it. Give me the names of the two guys on the ice that fled after you and your two pals went to check on Jimmy. I want names, addresses, where they hang, who might know where they are." Murdock pulled out his note pad and pen. Joe began to supply the requested information. To his surprise, Murdock was impressed with the detail that Sarkin was offering.

After fifteen minutes, Murdock stopped Sarkin. "Okay, I have enough. Now let's talk about your conversation with Sergeant Moody on the ice regarding Jake Farmer."

At first Sarkin looked confused so Murdock reminded him. "You were out on the ice having coffee and you started asking about Jake Farmer and how much time he had put in so far, and that he might be going after Moody when he gets out." Sarkin let out a breath of air. Murdock continued, "I want to know how you know Farmer and why you asked Sergeant Moody about him."

For a minute Sarkin stared at Murdock and said nothing. Murdock prodded him a little. "You know the prison keeps a file on everyone that visits every prisoner,…the day and time, the duration of the visit…everything…even phone calls. Just keep that in mind before you start talking."

Sarkin took another deep breath. "Okay, okay. I worked with Farmer on a few jobs where some big city guys were paying big bucks for venison…and deer heads with racks. The customer was bringing in big business partners from out in the mid-west. The venison was going for big money on the black market and the deer heads were just show pieces for a big sporting interest."

Murdock wrote in his notepad without looking up. "What was the name of the sporting interest?"

Sarkin paused. "Hey, now wait a minute. This is supposed to be about Farmer. You're gonna' get these big city dogs down on me too. I'm taking a chance with Farmer as it is."

Murdock looked up from his writing. "Okay, maybe we'll go there later. Who told you Farmer might be going after Moody when he gets out?" Sarkin said nothing and stared blankly at Murdock. Murdock waited and added,

"Look Joe, you give me this information or I'll tell the authorities you refused to talk at all. Your choice."

Sarkin shot right back at Murdock, "Farmer is one mean sonuvabitch when he gets pissed. If he ever finds out, you'll never find my body."

Murdock smiled weakly at Sarkin. "Other people went to see him, Joe. I'm sure he talked a big game to some of those people too."

Sarkin looked a little relieved. "Ya' think so?" Murdock raised his eyebrows and replied, "I told you before. We have records of every visitor."

The two men sat facing each other for several minutes without saying a word. Finally, Sarkin blurted it out, "Heard it from his brother-in law, Billy Jaggs. You know Billy is doing time in a different prison but he's talked to Jake on the phone a couple of times. I visited Billy once and he told me."

Murdock put his pad down. "So, you're saying you didn't hear it from Farmer himself."

Sarkin shook his head to indicate he didn't. "No way. I don't know Jake good enough to go visit him like that but I know Billy pretty good. He's the one that got me working with that crew from time to time."

Murdock pursed his lips and threw his pen down on the bed. Sarkin thought the gesture was aimed at him. "Hey, I needed the money…okay? I'm not saying it was proper."

Murdock ignored Sarkin and thought to himself, *Shit, it's only hearsay. He never saw Farmer and only heard it from a second party…not enough to hold up Farmer's parole hearing or even use against him.*

Murdock stood from his chair and gathered his things. "We're done here, Sarkin. Your cooperation will be noted but I think you ought to worry more about your leg than anything else." Murdock started for the door but stopped short and turned around to look at the confused Sarkin. "Just don't get your hopes up. The fact that you tried to kill a game warden still stands." Murdock turned and walked out the door.

Sarkin sat upright and shouted after the departing trooper, "Hey, what are you doing? You can't just leave. I told you what you wanted."

Murdock could hear Sarkin's words as he walked down the hall and stopped a nurse. "Excuse me Nurse, the man in Room 333 is making a lot of noise. Would you mind closing his door?" Murdock thanked her and turned the hall corner and made for the hospital's exit.

★★★★

CHAPTER 18

A week had passed since Tom Dooley's visit with Jake Farmer. The day was Wednesday, Jake's scheduled interview with the parole board. How he conducted himself and what he said in the next forty-five minutes would determine whether he would be granted a parole board hearing or not.

Jake stood nervously in front of his prison cell's sink preparing for his interview with the parole board. He finished dressing and combed his hair and wished he'd had a mirror. Inmates weren't allowed anything sharp or that could be made sharp in their cells. He craned his neck by the corner of his cell to get a look at the clock on the hallway wall. It was 10:45 AM. Jake stared at the clock. *In fifteen minutes I'll be standing in front of those pencil necks. I gotta' make a good first impression...have to look remorseful, like I'm sorry for what I did. Block out all my emotions.* Jake stopped and realized he had actually been trained by the very system that now wanted him to be truthful about how he felt, to put on an act when his inner emotions told him otherwise. Jake snickered to himself, *I'll use their own training against them.*

Jake heard the cell block's main door crack open. *Here they come. Let's do this.*

— — —

The Hearing Room was cold and barren. There were no pictures on the wall and no windows. The room was painted in a two-tone shade of dark green from floor to mid wall and a lighter green from there to the ceiling. Recessed rectangular lights were set in the dropped ceiling tiles emitting fluorescent light, brighter than the dingy white ceiling tiles that housed them.

Jake sat handcuffed in a lonely chair in the middle of the room set about ten feet away from a long table that served nine judicial administrators. Four men and five women sat at the table and eyed him curiously, judgmentally. A prison guard stood directly behind Jake, watching and waiting.

Jake took in his surroundings and tried to get comfortable with the situation. He smirked to himself as it reminded him of the oral board he had to sit in front of when he was testing for his game warden position thirty-seven years ago. *They didn't break me then and they won't break me now. I got this.*

The cold silence in the room was broken by a middle-aged woman who sat in the center of the nine people staring at him. "Good morning Mr. Farmer, I am Interviewer Pease. How are you feeling?"

He replied, "I'm feeling fine, Ma'am, thank-you." Jake noticed she had asked the question without cracking a smile. He looked at the rest of the panel. Everyone appeared stoic and unresponsive.

Interviewer Pease continued. "We are here this afternoon to discuss some concerns we have about rumors that have been generated about a feeling you may be harboring against your arresting officer, Sergeant Sam Moody." The woman stopped and stared blankly at Jake. "Do you understand the question and what it might be related to?"

Jake said nothing for a moment. He stared matter-of-factly back at the interviewer and thought, *That is an unfair question you old bag. She's trying to prejudice me on the first question, but I've got training here too.* Jake forced himself to remain calm. *I have to put her on the defensive. She doesn't know anything. She's just fishing…trying to get me to admit there could be rumors.*

Interviewer Pease addressed Jake again. "Mr. Farmer would you like me to repeat the question?"

Jake straightened up in his chair and replied, "No Ma'am, I was just making sure I had the question straight in my mind." Jake continued as he shared glances with the entire panel. "Begging your pardon Ma'am, but would you care to elaborate on what you call rumors? What you are asking could possibly include a wide variety of scenarios. Could you be more direct?"

Interviewer Pease jerked her head back in surprise and looked to her right and left. The other panel members ignored her questioning glances and continued to watch Jake. She cleared her throat and began again. "Mr. Farmer, Do you know a man by the name of Joe Sarkin?"

Jake nodded his head in a thoughtful way and looked back at her. "Yes, Ma'am, I believe I do. Not well, but he did work with my hunters on and off."

Pease wrote down some notes and looked back at Jake. "Did he come to visit you at any time during your incarceration?"

Jake made a frown while shaking his head. "Nope. Didn't really know him well enough. Like I said…he worked with my hunters sometimes."

Interviewer Pease nodded and looked to her right and nodded to the next Interviewer. "Mr. Jackson?"

George Jackson raised his eyebrows and met Jake's questioning look. "Uh, Mr. Farmer, I am Interviewer Jackson. We have it on good authority that you have said something to someone about possibly getting some revenge against the people or persons that had a hand in putting you here." He stared into Jake's eyes with seriousness and conviction. Jackson continued, "This interview has been organized and planned because of the seriousness of a threat that was heard by more than one person. We would like you to substantiate any credibility to these allegations."

Jake smiled at the panel and asked, "What allegations, sir?"

Jackson replied quickly, "Mr. Farmer!. Your cooperation in this matter may mean you get a parole hearing or not. Keep in mind, the idea of actual parole is not even a consideration at this time."

Jake shifted in his chair and cleared his throat. "I'm sorry if I've caused some frustration but Ms. Pease and yourself have both mentioned rumors. Please understand that I have been sequestered in a hospital for several months followed by ten months in a state penitentiary and have not been privy to a lot of …gossip." Jake paused and looked up and down the row of interviewers. He took in a breath, as if exasperated, and continued. "It's common knowledge that I was once a law enforcement officer and now I'm up for parole. I can believe there are probably a lot of rumors floating around but please don't ask me to incriminate myself by trying to guess at which one you are talking about."

Now, the entire panel all shared glances with one another. Finally, one member of the panel from the far left spoke into the microphone situated in front of him. "Jake Farmer, I am Bill Carson. I'm going to be right up front with you. I know what you did. I know how you compromised the department's trust as well as how our citizens look at officers, and personally I don't care if you ever get out of here." He paused for a moment and noticed the surprised look on Jake's face. Carson continued, "I am also aware of how you have been trained...as an officer, to avoid direct questioning and how to influence a conversation to your favor. I'm the boss here and if you don't start talking...right now, this hearing is over."

Jake's heart began to race. *The sonuvabitch has got some kind of special training. I gotta' do something quick.* Jake tried to hide his nervousness. "I'm sorry sir, if I came across that way. Without incriminating myself, I'm going to guess that you are speaking of a story my attorney mentioned to me." Jake paused for Carson to concur.

Carson nodded and said, "Continue."

Jake went on, "I heard a rumor too," and paused a moment for effect, "that my brother-in-law, Billy Jaggs, mentioned something about how pissed I am at Sergeant Moody for putting me in here. I won't lie to you. I have spoken to Billy on the phone once or twice in the last year, and I would be lying if I told you I wasn't angry with Sergeant Moody...but I don't think," and he looked back at the first interviewer, Ms. Pease, "that harboring ill feelings against someone can be considered revenge. The last conversation I had with Billy was over a month ago and I don't remember what the actual words were or why the topic came up but I haven't done anything except to complain about my captor. I can't be responsible for how another man, over the distance of miles, and over the telephone, may have construed what my meaning was." Jake paused and looked at the entire panel of men and women. "I think that is pretty normal behavior."

There was an awkward silence in the room and one of the other women interviewers asked, "Mr. Farmer, are you saying that your level of anger may have prompted you to say you would want to seek some sort of revenge on Sergeant Moody?"

Farmer smiled. "I told you I don't remember the entire conversation…only that it had gotten my dander up, and of course, I could have said something like that…in the heat of the moment. Anybody would have."

One after the other, the remaining interviewers had their chance with Jake. Jake kept them all at bay by being vague but reasonable with his answers, careful not to indicate that he was not beyond fault.

Finally, Bill Carson slapped the table with his hand. "Okay, Mr. Farmer. Your hour has come to an end. You will be notified when we have made our decision." Carson looked across the room. "Guard, please take Mr. Farmer back to his cell."

The guard collected Jake and ushered him from the room. When the hearing room door closed behind them, the panel shared their opinions of the last hour and what their observations of the former game warden turned poacher were. The panel deliberated for another hour. Jake's Parole board hearing was granted.

★★★★

CHAPTER 19

P eg was busy cleaning the cabin, the boys had left for school an hour ago, and Sam had left long ago an early morning patrol in the West Hills Territory. She was looking forward to a whole day with no men around. Maybe she could finally get something done around the cabin.

She had started her cleaning in the boys' bedrooms upstairs. She was working up a sweat making the beds, picking toys up off the floors and vacuuming. Peg had turned the stereo up high so she could hear it while she worked. The rooms were a mess. The boys' desks were cluttered with everything but school materials. Fishing and hiking equipment were everywhere. Unraveled sleeping bags were stuffed under one of the beds. She promised herself she'd have a talk with those boys when they got home tonight.

Sam was no better. Uniforms worn more than once still hung in the closet. *Why can't he just put these in the laundry when they're dirty? I end up having to wash everything all at once. Sometimes he's just like a big kid. He's getting a talking-to tonight also.*

Peg rooted around in the back of Sam's closet trying to pull his extra pair of jungle boots out into the daylight. *Can't believe it*, she thought. *Dried mud all over the bottoms! I'm going to remind him we have a porch for stuff like this.*

Exasperated, Peg straightened up and took a breath of air. Exhaling in frustration, she put her hands on her hips and snapped her head to the side to flip her long hair out of her face. As she did, she caught a glimpse of something outside the window that faced the front of the cabin. As she turned back toward the closet her mind's eye stopped her. *What was that outside the cabin?* Peg looked back out the window and up the long gravel driveway. A red pick-up truck was parked on the opposite side of the street.

She stared at the truck for a moment. A man sat in the driver's seat, not moving, not even looking in her direction. Peg straightened up and cocked her head back with her chin sticking out. *Who could that be? There's nothing around here to look at or wait for…just fields and forest.*

Peg watched the truck for a few more minutes. The driver brought a cup or thermos of something to his mouth and took a drink. Still no glance in the direction of the cabin. *Maybe he's broken down and waiting for a tow truck*, she thought. Satisfied with that thought Peg decided to go back to her cleaning and check on the truck in a little while. She looked at her watch. It was 9:30 in the morning.

Time had passed quickly and Peg had forgotten about the truck at the end of her driveway. She was vacuuming the living room when she decided to take a break and check on the truck. Peg looked at her watch. It was now 11:00. She walked over to one of the porch windows. The driver still sat there sipping on something. *Who is that? I've seen that truck before.* Peg went to the hall closet to retrieve Sam's extra pair of binoculars. Hurrying back to the window she raised the binoculars to her face and looked back up the driveway. Her fingers fiddled with the focus knobs and suddenly a familiar face filled the binocular's lens. Peg stood back in surprise and dropped the binoculars to the floor. "Farmer!"

Peg shouted the name aloud as if she was calling to someone in the house…but no one else was home. Peg stood at the window wondering what she should do. Should she call Sam? No, she remembered he was on an early patrol and unavailable anyway. She stole a quick glance back out the window to see where the family dog was. *Where is traveler?*

Traveller sat on the front of the porch watching the truck. *Oh, thank God! He sees him. At least I know he'll bark and maybe intimidate Farmer if he tries to get out and approach the house.*

Peg sat down at the kitchen table and considered the situation for what it was. If she called the Police Department, they would ask what he was doing and she would have to say he hadn't done anything but park across the street. He was parked on state property in his own truck. They would think she was getting paranoid and wouldn't come out anyway. Then Peg started to get angry and she spoke aloud. "I'm not going to let the likes of that bastard scare me in my own home!" With that peg stepped over to the Porch door and walked out onto the open porch.

Peg slowly pushed the wooden screen door open and passed through the door way. As she walked slowly out onto the porch floor, she held her hands cupped over her mouth. The screen door slammed closed behind her. At that moment the driver in the red truck turned and looked right at Peg as she stood in the middle of the porch. He stared at her for a few moments then smiled. The driver turned away, started his truck, and drove away slowly.

Peg was so frightened she felt as if she couldn't move. She willed herself to get back into the house. *Have to get back inside the house. He could be coming down the drive any moment…or what if he's got friends with him…what if they're somewhere around the house? MOVE YOUR LEGS!*

Slowly, stiffly, Peg shuffled backwards. Her hands covered her mouth. She forced herself to look to the right. There was nothing by the barn that she could see. Slowly she looked to the left...nothing by the woods. Her head was shaking, her respiration was escalated and it felt as if her heart would come through her chest. A cold chill crawled up her back. Peg wanted to shout but all that came from her mouth was a few garbled sobs. It was a feeling of total helplessness.

Traveller watched Peg as she edged backward toward the open screen door. Peg caught sight of Traveller in her peripheral vision. "Traveller. Come here, boy." Traveller stood and trotted over to Peg and sat down in front of her. He Looked up into Peg's eyes and wagged his tail. Peg relaxed a little at the sight of the dog. It reinforced the fact she was not alone. "Traveller...in the house." Traveller brushed by Peg's leg and waited by the half open screen door. Peg turned and ran the next three steps to the door, flung it out of her way and stepped inside the cabin. She leaned against the wall of the kitchen just inside the door and tried to calm herself. Traveller followed her in and sat by her feet.

I thought Farmer had another year to go...at least six months more. It was supposed to be something like two years of time after getting out of the hospital.

Peg's breathing had started to ease up. She took deep breaths and tried to regain her composure. Finally, she knelt down and looked into Traveller's eyes. He gave her a complimentary lick on the end of her nose. It was so sudden and innocent, the gesture caused her to let out a small laugh. Traveller continued to wag his tail. She laughed again and patted him on the head. "You're a good boy, Trav. You stay right with me. I've got to sit down." Traveller followed her over to the kitchen table. Peg sat down and leaned forward with her elbows on the table, her head in her hands, and began to sob.

Peg tried to reason with the situation and spoke aloud. "He's supposed to be in jail." Peg lifted her head from her hands. "Wait…am I over-reacting? Could it have been someone else?" She thought for a moment. *I know I've been thinking about Sam's enemies too much lately. It was probably just some guy making a call on the side of the road or checking his road map.* Suddenly, the screen door flew open causing Peg to scream. Traveller stood and turned to the open kitchen door.

"Hey, what's the matter, Honey?" It was Sam. Peg turned to see who it was and ran into his arms. He held her while she sobbed against his shirt.

Sam could see the fright in his wife. He could feel it as she leaned into his body. This behavior was not part of the woman he knew. Whatever had frightened her must have been extreme. He slowly stroked her back and held her tight with the other arm. Eventually, when her sobs subsided, he asked, "What's going on, Peg? What happened? Everything is okay."

Peg looked up at him and glared at him for a moment, then slammed both her fists into his chest several times. Sam stood back while getting hold of her flailing arms. "Okay, okay. I'm here, Peg. I've got you." Peg began to slow down, her strength waning. She was out of breath again. Sam saw she was coming around and asked, "Honey, what has gotten into you?"

She glared at him again. "What has gotten into me? What has gotten into us? She paused and blurted, "Jake Farmer!"

Sam slowly walked her back to the table and sat her down. "That's why I came home early, Peg. The P.D. called. Jake is out on parole."

— — —

Peg and Sam sat at the kitchen table for a long while. Neither said a word. They just sat and stared at the table. Both knew there was a problem, a problem that had had been building for a long while. Now the problem was working its way into the family. The fear of revenge from wrong doers that Sam had dealt with in the past. They never thought it could entwine itself into such a sacred and special place as their own family.

Sam sat at the table comfortable to just keep Peg company. He was ready to talk when she was. He wanted to wait for her to get through whatever frightened her. It took about twenty minutes before she spoke. Finally, without lifting her gaze from the table she said, "Sam, I'm done. I can't do this anymore."

Sam reached across the table and held her hand. "I know you've been through something that has terrified you. I know it's because of me…because of what I do, and I'm sorry it's come to this but this is something we've already talked about."

Peg looked up and into his eyes. "Sam, this has gone too far. Farmer is out and watching our house! It's a good thing the boys are at school! This is a huge threat to our family… our way of life. I don't want it!" She drew her hand away from his.

Sam's heart sunk. He felt his heart breaking. "Peg, you're very upset right now. We can talk this whole thing out."

She looked away from him and glanced out the window. After a moment she said, "Farmer was here, Sam. He sat in his truck at the end of our driveway and waited for me to see him. When he saw that I did, he drove off. Not fast, but slowly…like there's more to come."

Sam nodded his head. "This is what he wants, Peg. His game is to intimidate us. He knows he can park on state property all day and is not trespassing. His idea is to scare you and make you wonder what he's up to…let your imagination get the better of you." Peg looked back into Sam's eyes. He continued, "Farmer is going to try to destroy the Moody family. Not necessarily in the physical sense but by instilling fear of the unknown into you and the boys… and so far, it's working."

Peg stood from the table and shook her head. "I know, I know. He really got to me, okay? All I could think of was what if he did this when the boys were home." She began to walk around the kitchen and waved her hand in a large circle. "He's a threat to all of this…everything we've worked for…everything we have."

Sam stayed seated at the table. "Peg, you were a probation officer. I have to say I'm a little surprised at your reaction."

Peg turned quickly and glared at Sam. After a few moments she collected herself. "Yes, I was a probation officer and I know what can happen in these cases. It's different when it's your own family that is the target."

Sam nodded his head. "I can understand that but we are way beyond running from this thing. We need to think it out and reason with it." Peg was still pacing the kitchen floor.

Suddenly she stopped and looked straight at Sam. "Why didn't you call me when you first heard he was out?"

Sam stood from the table. "I did Peg. I called three times. When I didn't get you the first time, I jumped into my cruiser and called you twice on my way here." It was only then that Peg realized she had been vacuuming the house and couldn't have heard the phone. The look on her face was utter surprise and remorse. It was the kind of shock that one didn't think oneself capable of. She had panicked.

She dropped her head and walked up to her husband, burying her face in his chest and began to cry. "I'm sorry." She looked up at Sam. "I don't know if I can handle this."

Sam held her tight. "We'll handle it, Honey." He looked down at her and said, "We'll handle it together. We have to," and bent his head down so his cheek was pressed against hers.

★★★★

CHAPTER 20

A fter Sam and Peg had talked things over and Peg was thinking more rationally, Sam had made a call to the Thompson Police Department notifying them of the incident. They promised they would have a cruiser parked by Sam's property, 24/7 and send an extra patrol by every hour for the next two weeks.

The next morning, Sam was on his way back to the Thompson P.D. to discuss Jake Farmer's stalking activity of yesterday. Even with the increased security around the Moody's residence, Sam was still reluctant to leave the house to discuss the incident with Thompson's law enforcement administration. Peg assured Sam she was okay and would be fine. The boys were back at school and hadn't been told about the incident.

As he drove, he began to think back on yesterday's stalking incident. It bothered him deeply that because of him, a lowlife like Jake Farmer was able to drive to his home and terrify his wife merely by making a presence. Sam began to think that Farmer's appearance may be merely a bluff or in the worst case a warning. At any rate, Sam felt it was a definite act to frighten the Moody family. Sam knew the authorities were going to listen to his complaints but in the end, were going to say that Farmer hadn't as yet broken any laws, wasn't on the Moody's property, and drove away when he saw that Peg noticed him.

Sam began to get angry. *These laws, this job…who does it protect? I did my part in putting that guy away for most of the crimes he committed and what do they do…let him out early so he can harass my family when he gets out. My wife is ready to leave me because of what I do, and my entire way of life as well as my family's has changed.*

Soon the gates of the Thompson police department filled Sam's windshield. Sam was surprised. He must have been in such deep thought he never noticed the scenery or anything else between his cabin and the P.D. He pulled into his usual place, got out of his truck and walked into the station.

A group of officials sat awaiting Sam's arrival in the large meeting room down the hall from Lieutenant Alban's office. Sam opened the door and walked in. Seated at the head of a long oak table was the Thompson Police Chief, William Harrison. Seated at the far end of the table was Thompson's Deputy Chief Paul Bingham, State Parole Board Officer, Bill Carson, and Joe Hardy, Chief of Detectives. Fish and Game Captain John Fletcher and Fish and Game Lieutenant Gene Alban occupied the other side.

The Police Chief greeted Sam as he stepped inside the room. "Good morning Sergeant Moody. Please come in and take a seat. Help yourself to the coffee on the table." Sam nodded at the table of officials and sat down next to Alban.

Sam explained the scenario of what had transpired at his home the day before and pointed out that Peg had already given a statement to the officer that came out to his house after Sam called in the incident. The room was quiet for a moment when the Chief addressed Sam. "We're very sorry this has happed Sam but we don't know what it really was yet. We are going to need to speak with your wife when she's ready but for now we'll respond to the matter at hand." Sam nodded his head to indicate he understood. The Chief went on, "As you know we have patrols surveilling your house 24/7 and will keep that up until we speak to Mr. Farmer."

Bill Carson interrupted the Chief. "Excuse me Chief, I'd like to interject something." The Chief nodded and Carson looked across the table at Sam. "Sergeant Moody. Please be advised we appreciate your efforts in bringing Mr. Farmer to justice and gave his parole considerable thought before allowing it. All indications from his answers and behavior during the interview and then again at the parole board hearing gave us no indication he might be looking toward a vendetta of any kind. We have his probation officer trying to locate him at this moment and when he is found will be brought in to answer further questions as to why he was in the vicinity of your property." Carson continued to stare at Moody as if waiting for an acknowledgement. Sam returned his gaze without emotion.

Chief Harrison began again. "Sam please understand we notified you as soon as was appropriate without compromising Mr. Farmer's constitutional rights." Sam remained quiet.

An awkwardness consumed the room and Captain Fletcher addressed the parties at the conference table. "Gentlemen, this is all very…considerate of you but I don't think you have as yet grasped the gravity of the situation." Fletcher looked around the table. "You need to understand you have a highly trained Fish and Game officer with more experience in forest attack and survival tactics than most of my game wardens. He has an intimate knowledge of Thompson's terrain and waterways. In addition to all of that, he knows how we operate as a law enforcement agency which makes us as law enforcement…vulnerable. If he is considering revenge on Sergeant Moody, we will have our hands full."

Lieutenant Alban let the room absorb Fletcher's words and added, "Farmer knows our patrol times and areas and who is assigned to those areas. We all realize, that in his mind, there is good reason for Farmer to lean in the dark direction because…Sergeant Moody has had a hand in making a considerable change in Farmer's life."

Bill Carson responded. "What are you trying to say, Lieutenant?" Carson paused for effect, "…that we've released some sort of monster?"

Alban answered quickly. "I'm saying you gave a prisoner his constitutional rights without considering the damage he may be capable of based on a couple of hour-long sessions. It's been twenty-four hours since he scared the hell out of Mrs. Moody and you still haven't been able to hook up with him."

The discussion was getting more and more heated. Finally, Chief Harrison brought the room to order. "Alright, alright, gentlemen. Let's calm down." He looked down the table to where Sam sat. "Sergeant Moody, you have been very quiet. I'd like to know your take on all of this." Everyone turned to look at Sam.

Sam nodded his head in answer to the Chief and then looked across the table at Bill Carson. "I suggest you find your boy Farmer, quick. If I feel as if he is a threat to my family or my home and property, I will not hesitate to react." Sam stood up from the table and left the room.

Alban looked at the two Chiefs and Carson and raised his eyebrows. "Better do as he says. He means it."

★★★★

CHAPTER 21

S am left the police station and drove toward the East Hills territory, just northeast of his cabin. He felt frustrated and angry as he drove. He felt like the meeting he just left was all lip service. The state was going to do right by Farmer's constitutional rights and the police department didn't tell him anything he didn't already know. Why was the Chief going down that road anyway? The three Fish and Game officers in that room knew what Farmer knew, his training, and what he was capable of. It was all a show for the State. Sam felt he would have to be the one to ensure Farmer never gets near his family. *First I'm going up to Lee's cabin in the High Meadow. Lee will tell me if there is any scuttlebutt about Farmer's plans, if there is any.*

Sam began to calm down as he drove. The thought that he still had an ally he could count on, one that would be unbiased and not have to play any political games, was calming. Lee had been there for him before and Sam knew he could count on him again if need be. Sam's thoughts drifted back to how he had met his old friend, how they had hunted and fished together…everything they had learned and been through together.

Suddenly all the good thoughts that had flooded his mind disappeared and a sudden rush of anxiety and guilt filled his consciousness. He realized he hadn't seen or spoken to Lee since that night in the poacher's field in New Hampshire. *Shit! It's been over a year! How could I have let that go so long?* Sam tried to rationalize his reasons for not checking on his old buddy. *Well, I know how much Lee likes his privacy and under the circumstances I did want to put some time between us after that ambush we pulled on Farmer's poaching ring. If anyone ever found out he was an accomplice to a state Fish and Game sting, we'd both be finished. I'd be done as a game warden and his business as a hunting and fishing guide would be over and he'd be serving time.*

Sam felt embarrassed. He had let it go too long. What must Lee be thinking? Sam satisfied himself that maybe subconsciously, he did it for Lee. There could be no loose ends on how that ambush ended. As far as the state law enforcement administration and state judicial system were concerned, it was a closed case. No one ever saw Lee or knew he'd been there. Sam reminded himself that he had given Lee a choice right before the ambush and Lee chose to continue as a volunteer. But what about now? Sam needed him again and hadn't so much as paid him a visit up in his High Meadow. Would Lee feel as though he was being used or would he understand? He thought about the situation over and over as he headed for the East Hills Territory. Finally, Sam decided that the situation was as it is. Lee would have to understand.

— — —

Sam pulled into the little clearing at the base of the East Hills. He got out of his truck and panned the area. *This place never changes*, he thought. *Beautiful! I hope it stays this way.* He locked the truck and turned toward the wooded path that would take him to Lee's cabin. It would be about a two-hour walk, some of it steep and rough, but it would be good to see his old friend again.

Sam finally crested a small ridge and looked down into a shallow basin tucked into the side of the mountain. He smiled as he saw Lee's cabin in the distance. The field was open as usual with a few goats grazing. Sam stepped forward to begin his descent into the basin when something poked him in the back. It felt like a stiff rod...hard and round. A muffled voice from behind murmured, "Hold it right there." Sam froze in his tracks. The voice came again. "Put your hands where I can see 'em and turn around." Sam complied. Then a smiling Lee Sparks stood staring into Sam's face holding a walking stick. He wore a bandana across his mouth. "Gotcha'…you're dead."

Sam dropped his hands and felt his shoulders drop. "You sonuvabitch! You know better than to play that game with me. I could have pulled a knife or…"

Lee cut him off. "I got ya', pal. You'd be dead if I wanted it that way." The two old friends stood for a moment not saying a word, then each of them allowed a slight smile, followed by a short chuckle. Sam put his hand out to shake and Lee grabbed it and squeezed hard. Lee hadn't changed. The tall, lean woodsman was a little taller than Sam at six foot-two inches tall. He still kept his long, jet black hair at shoulder length and his long black mustache came to a pointed end at each jawbone. The familiar smile adorned a long thin face, tanned and weathered, from consistent exposure to the elements.

Lee leaned on the walking stick. "So, what brings Sam Moody up so high in the hills? What's going on?"

Sam smiled and nodded his head, "Farmer."

Lee took a step forward and put his hand on the back of Sam's shoulder. "Yeah, I've been expecting you. Let's go down to the cabin and talk about it. I've already got a pot of coffee goin.' Saw you coming up path about an hour ago." Sam smiled and nodded as they descended the lip of the basin.

— — —

Sam and Lee sat at the hand-hewn kitchen table sipping coffee. The cabin's interior was a little dark as there was no electricity. The only illumination came from the windows in the cabin's walls. Lee sat across from Sam in front of the fieldstone fireplace. He leaned back in his handmade chair and rested one boot on the fireplace hearth. As usual, Lee said nothing as Sam told the story of last winter with Sarkin, the rumors, Farmer's parole, and his suspected stalking incident at the Moody's cabin. When he finished, he took a gulp of his coffee and waited for Lee's comments. Lee was a stoic individual and it was no surprise to Sam that it might be a while before Lee gave his impression.

Lee took another sip from his mug of coffee, turned toward the fireplace, grabbed a poker, and stirred the fire a bit. "Where's Farmer now?"

"Don't know, Lee. Nobody knows...not even his parole officer. He's out there somewhere and I think he's looking to intimidate. Probably wants some revenge."

Lee just nodded his head. "Revenge? You think he wants revenge, Sam?" Lee jerked his head sharply from the fire and glared at Sam. "Of course, he's gonna' want to make you pay. In his mind, you are responsible for ruining his life." He paused a moment to let that sink in, then continued. "I know you expected this and I know that's not why you came to see me. Tell me why you're really here."

Sam stood from the table and walked around the kitchen with his coffee. He told Lee about the meeting with Thompson's law enforcement administration and the state's Judicial Services. "I walked out of that meeting, Lee. Left Alban and Fletcher sitting there with those people from the State. From what they said, it sounds like they are more concerned about an ex-con's constitutional rights than anything else."

Lee watched Sam as he paced the kitchen floor. "And what are you thinking, Sam?"

Sam stopped and looked at Lee. "I have a wife and three young boys. I can't assume Farmer is going to rehabilitate like they'd expect him to. I'll do what I have to for the safety of my family."

Lee motioned Sam back to the table with a shake of his head. "Come on back here and sit down. We need a plan." Sam complied and dropped into the chair across from Lee. "Farmer is a clever guy, Sam. I've been hearing some scuttlebutt all through these hills…from the trappers, the hunters, even the taxidermists. Some of it may have even been leaked by the cabin people in the West Hills Territory. Whatever…the word is that Farmer is coming for you."

Sam allowed a frown like it wasn't the first time someone fresh out of prison had made such a threat. He looked back into his coffee. "I don't think that's too clever of him…going around telling people he's going after the guy who put him in jail."

Lee slammed his coffee mug down on the solid oak table. "Damn it, Sam! You know how dangerous this guy is. Can't you see what he's doing?" Sam looked up surprised at Lee's reaction. Lee continued, "He lets it leak out that he's gonna' get Sam Moody back. Farmer knows people are gonna' take that and run with it, and every time that little bit of information gets passed along, it gets changed a little bit more, until the original story is nothing like the one that people are hearing now. Farmer knows that eventually, the story, in its worst form, is going to get to you."

Sam nodded his head in affirmance, "Like last winter's ice fishing bust with Joe Sarkin."

Lee leaned across the table toward Sam. "Don't you see? He hasn't done anything yet, but he's got you walking out of meetings, threatening his welfare, and worried enough to come all the way up here to see me."

Sam shot back, "He parked across the street from my house until he knew my wife saw him…two days after he was out of prison! He had no reason to be out in my area!"

Lee leaned back in his chair, "And what did he do then, Sam?" Sam didn't answer. Lee answered for him. "He drove away slowly. Lee paused for effect. "Slowly, Sam."

Sam thought for a moment. "To me that's like a warning to her. Like, I'm leaving but I'll be back."

Lee stood from the table and shook his head in disagreement. "No, no, no. He's working on your nerves ole' buddy. He knows the most important thing to you is your family and that is what he's going to go after first. If he can get you away from a rational way of thinking by attacking your emotions, he knows you're more likely to do something you normally wouldn't. His plan is to get you in an unbalanced state where you're most vulnerable. He has to, Sam. He knows how good you are in the woods and he needs an advantage."

Sam finally shook his head in agreement. "Okay, what's your plan?"

Lee smiled and sat back down at the table. He picked up the coffee pot and filled both of their mugs. "First we need to decide what we're going to do with Peg and the kids." They talked all afternoon.

★★★★

CHAPTER 22

J ake Farmer's attitude about who he was and how everything had turned out was getting better. His thought process was still all about himself and how others had caused his life to be turned upside down. His health had improved and was almost back to normal, he had coerced the state judicial system into shortening his actual time in prison, and best of all, he had scared the wits out of Sam's wife with an impromptu visit to the family's cabin. Jake sat on his old deck at his house by the river. He sipped a beer as he watched the water flow by and remembered happier times. He thought of his youth and all the special hours he had spent with friends, here by the same river he now watched.

The breeze from the river periodically wafted up to where Jake sat and rearranged his white but still thick hair. He took another swig from his beer can and looked about his neglected yard. The place had gotten pretty rundown in the time he'd been away. At least, a few of the cabin people had felt sorry for him and come down from the West Hills to mow the lawn once in a while. The grass was more like hay, the bushes that bordered his property had grown wild, and several kinds of ivy had begun to lay claim to the house's foundation walls.

Eventually, his thoughts drifted back to the matter at hand. Summer was fast approaching and he had to get phase two of his plan started. He knew where Sam's patrol area was and had to get out there to look it over. He smiled that Sam's rank actually would help his purpose since Sergeants had to patrol all the territories from time to time.

Jake looked back out over the river and started to consider some of his best plans. He could set up snares in the woods. He knew Sam's patrol areas so it would be easy to get him tangled up in some rope…maybe hanging from a tree. Jake stopped to picture that for a moment and smiled. *Yeah, Moody hanging upside down in the woods while I sit in front of him, telling him what I'm going to do to him and then to his family.* Jake smiled even broader as he imagined the look on Sam's face when he told him. He lit a cigarette and blew a puff of smoke out into the air. *Why don't I just make it easy and just kill the sonuvabitch. One shot, one bullet to the head… and it's over. I'll just borrow Billy's rifle and let 'em have it.* Jake took another pull on the cigarette and shook his head from side to side. *Nah, I can't just kill him. I need to see him squirm first. That's part of the revenge. I have to see to it that he pays for everything he's done to me.*

Jake sat back in his rocking chair and continued to ponder his alternatives. Suddenly he stopped rocking and sat straight up. *I need to continue the intimidation game. By now he knows I've been over to his cabin and scared his wife. He's probably wondering about my next move so I'm gonna' wait a little. Spring Turkey season will be starting soon. I'll follow him into the woods, wait to see which trail he takes, and find the high ground for that area. Better yet, I'll get one of the cabin people to follow him and call me so I can get a head start. I'll jump on one of the spurs (an access path) to that trail. Once I know which trail he's gonna' take I'll know which hunting area he's gonna' check, and circle around to get the drop on him.*

Jake started rocking in his chair again while nodding his head up and down. *Yeah, that's it! I'll borrow Billy's .30-30 rifle with the scope. If things haven't changed, Sam will be going into the North Woods area by the Massachusetts border. I'm gonna' figure on that. I'll get some of the cabin people to watch all the likely areas. When they spot him, they can call me and I can go in from the opposite direction to head him off.* Jake smiled and sat back in his rocking chair again. *I didn't spend all that time in prison studying those damn topo maps for nothing. I know the back ways into every part of this territory.*

★★★★

CHAPTER 23

S pring had finally arrived in Thompson's North Woods hills and it was Opening Day for Spring Turkey Season. Jake Farmer sat in his Dodge pick-up truck. It was 5:05 AM and Jake knew legal hunting hours had begun thirty minutes earlier. He peered through his windshield and scanned the dark, makeshift, clearing. *Don't expect anyone would be coming in this way to get to the ravine. Climbing that cutline is gonna' be a little tough. If there is anyone is on the other side of the ridge at this hour, It's gonna' take them a while to get their gear together and get out to the ravine. That'll give me time to get up that old cutline over there and get into position on the ledge. Mr. 'By the Book', Sam friggin' Moody will let them hunt a little before he checks 'em, and by the time he finishes checking their paperwork and ammo, I'll be up on the ledge waiting.*

Jake looked over at the dark opening to the cutline. *It ought to take me about thirty minutes to climb through that. If I get to a good spot above the ravine's trailhead by 6:00 AM, I'll be in good position to see Sammy walk into the ravine.*

Jake had driven down an old tobacco road that he knew was a rear access to one of the best turkey hunting areas in the region. He parked his truck's tailgate up against the wood line and shut off the engine. Jake pulled out his topographical map and turned on his mini mag lite. Just as he had planned; the hills rose up steeply behind his truck and

117

leveled out onto a ridge facing north to the Massachusetts border. The turkey hunting area lay in a small ravine on the north side of the ridge so Jake would have to climb the south side to get to the ridge. It would be hard travelling from where he had parked the truck but there were still some old cut lines that he could use to get close to a ledge that overlooked the main path to the ravine.

He folded the map and stuffed it into a camouflaged day pack that he had on the front seat. Next, he opened the front of the day pack and checked his ammo pouch. There was one .30-30 rifle cartridge, an extra clip for his nine-millimeter pistol, and a small roll of duct tape in the back of the compartment for blisters and quick repairs. In the main part of the pack was a set of binoculars, a pair of shooting gloves, an extra hunting knife, one water bottle, and a thermos of coffee. Jake reached inside his hunting vest and felt for his nine-millimeter under his left arm. He smiled and gave it a gentle pat. Finally, he checked his wristwatch. *Thirty-five minutes to sunup. Better get up that hill. If I know Moody, he'll be coming down that path right after six o'clock so he can check hunters on their way into the ravine.* He leaned back against his seat's headrest and drew a sigh of relief. *What a break! Good thing one of Billy's cabin people heard that rumor about Moody patrolling this area today. That little bit of info is gonna' save me a lot of time and effort.*

Jake opened the door and stepped out. He reached into the cab and pulled out his day pack and slipped it on. Jake looked around the abandoned clearing. No one around. He reached into the cab area behind the driver's seat and pulled out Billy's rifle. The scope had been adjusted the night before. He threw the rifle over his shoulder and adjusted the shoulder strap against his chest. *I better get up on that ridge before anyone sees me with this. It would be just like some do-gooder-hunter to call in and report someone carrying a rifle on Opening Day for spring turkey season.* Jake scanned the area again. *This has got to be quick, clean and quiet. Get in...get out. I'll ditch the rifle before I come down.*

Jake turned back to his truck and gently closed the door. He threw back his shoulders, stretched, and made for the surveyor's cut line. *I'm back*, he thought.

— — —

It was dark as Jake made his way through the old cutline. It wasn't really a path, but a roughly hacked corridor through the dense forest to access specific landmarks. Cut saplings and brush still protruded six to eight inches from the soil from which they emerged. Some of the sapling's cut shafts resembled punji sticks and had severely sharp points cut at an angle from the random use of a machete or bush hook. Jake kept flipping his mag lite on to ensure he was following the roughly cut corridor. Now and again, he stumbled on what was left of a tree or plant growth of several years ago. Following such a corridor in the dark was difficult, especially with an ever-steepening incline.

Jake's respiration was up and he was out of breath. The walking was difficult and the angle of incline increased with every step he took. He leaned against a tree and took out a bottle of water from his day pack. He was sweating profusely. Jake took a long pull from the bottle and tried to catch his breath. *Damn Moody. Every time I get involved with him there's always pain and suffering that comes with it. Every friggin' time!*

Jake's breathing began to slow and his heart rate began to calm. He glanced at his wrist watch...It was 5:30 AM. He'd only been hiking fifteen minutes. He looked up through the gray, naked trees, *Sunup. It's almost time. I gotta' get to that ledge before Moody gets into the ravine.*

Jake stuffed the water bottle back into his day pack and began to walk again. Evidently, a loose vine or piece of scrub brush had gotten tangled with his left boot when he had stopped to lean against the tree. Jake tripped and fell face down onto the old cutline. He felt a hot searing pain in his right side as he struggled to collect himself in the darkness. The muzzle of his rifle slammed against the back of his head causing some dizziness. "Fuck," Jake shouted his anxiety into the cool, black air of the morning. He slowly got to his feet and began to stand. He grimaced in pain and reached for his right side. It felt as if he'd been stuck in the ribs with a knife.

Jake pulled his hand back from under his hunting vest and pulled off his hunting glove. Then he carefully reached back in to feel what was causing the pain. His hand felt wet and slippery. Jake cursed aloud again. "Damn cutline!" One of the sharp saplings had penetrated his vest and right side just below the armpit. Jake gently poked at it and felt for the hole. His heart began to race a little until he shined his mag lite on the wound. The sharp stick had penetrated his flesh but deflected off one of his upper ribs. He inspected the wound as he noted the blood exiting. Jake spoke aloud as if he were reporting the damage to someone, "Doesn't look too deep. Just a flesh wound." He reached into his day pack and took out some tissue and a small roll of duct tape. He wiped the blood from the wound and inadvertently dropped the bloody tissue on the ground. Quickly, Jake ripped a piece of duct tape from its roll and stretched it across his exposed skin. He cut a second length as if to make an X across the wound and spoke aloud. "Damn tape works for foot blisters…should at least stop the bleeding for a while."

Satisfied that he had stifled the situation for at least the time being, he stuffed the tape back in his pack. Then he straightened up and continued to head for the ridge's summit.

The sky began to show its colorful hues as sunrise approached. The dark, unfriendly sky with gray clouds appeared to float away as the bright yellows and orange rays pushed up from below the ridge's east side. Jake checked his watch, *5:40. I've got twenty minutes to get into position.*

Jake walked for ten more minutes and noticed the incline was beginning to flatten out. He smiled to himself as this was an indication that he was nearing the top of the ridge.

Finally, the tree line appeared with open air on the other side. He had arrived. *Now to find that ledge.*

━ ━ ━

Lee Sparks was also aware of the several spurs and access trails that led to the ravine's ledge area. In line with his plan with Sam to stifle Farmer, Lee had spent the night in the North Woods area just south of the ravine. He had picked a secluded campsite that provided a clear view of the access road south of the North Woods Ridge. The campsite was north and above the main access road to the area where an old dirt road and clearing still remained. The plan had been to let Lee leak Sam's patrol assignment for Opening Day with the hope that the rumor would get passed along in hunting circles that planned to use that area.

Lee's camp provided an excellent view of the entire south side of the North Woods area. He sat watching the area at 4 AM while his coffee brewed over a small portable Peak camp stove. A fire would have been out of the question as it would have easily given away his position in the dark woods. When a large Dodge pick-up truck turned down the old access road, Lee extinguished the burner's stove and grabbed his night vision binoculars. As anticipated, the truck's marker plate revealed that it was Jake Farmer's truck heading down the old dirt road to the clearing at the south side of the North Woods ridge line. Lee dropped the binoculars to his chest, *Time to go.*

— — —

Lee looked at his wristwatch. It was 5:05 AM. He figured he was about a half mile from the access road and two hundred feet higher in elevation. His plan was to get to the bottom of the ridge's south side in the next twenty minutes. He had the steep incline to help speed his descent but silence was still a priority. Lee knew Jake would be checking his equipment which might buy him some time to get to the clearing's edge. The idea was to let Jake keep a small lead so he wouldn't know he was being followed.

Lee stood from his crouch and reached for his .300 mag high powered rifle and slung it behind his right shoulder. He was dressed in brown camouflaged BDUs with a Vietnam War era slouch hat to match. Brown jungle boots covered his feet and were useful for light walking or running. A light brown garrison belt wrapped his waist with spare ammo cases for his rifle and a six-inch military combat knife hung from his right side. The blade was blackened to keep it from shining in the moonlight. He reached into his daypack and pulled out his mini binoculars, placed its lanyard around his neck, and stuffed them into his BDU shirt pocket. He felt for his mini mag lite and found it at its usual place above his left hip. He was ready to go. Lee turned to look at his lonely camp in the side of the hill. He poured himself a cup of the freshly brewed coffee, took a couple of quick swallows and threw the remaining liquid into the nearby brush. Satisfied he had everything, Lee started down the steep slope.

★★★★

CHAPTER 24

Jake stepped through the tree line onto a flat rock area with various tumbles of scrub brush that protruded from its cracks and crevices. He reached up and wiped his forehead with his right wrist as he looked out over the ravine. One hundred feet below, the ravine sported a fairly flat area about a quarter mile wide with a sand and gravel floor. More scrub brush and saplings dotted the area. Jake looked northwest along the ravine to a wood line where an opening to a trailhead revealed itself. He smiled and thought, *There it is. Moody should be entering the ravine right there*. Jake estimated the distance to the trailhead at about three hundred feet from where he stood. *That's too long a shot with the vertical angle. I gotta' get closer.*

Jake took a sip from his water bottle and began to walk the ridge making sure to stay toward the tree line so his silhouette wouldn't be seen against the dawning day. It was fairly flat on the ledge and its vertical position offered no obstacles in front of the ravine below. Then he saw it. The perfect vantage point. There was a natural rock outcropping that extended out over the edge of the ledge that was flat and about two feet tall. He could position his rifle on that natural table and still be hidden from below.

Jake walked up to the table, unslung his rifle, and stripped off his pack. Then he sat down, leaned against the rock surface, and pulled off his hunting vest to check his aching side. The bleeding had stopped but the wound was a continual, nagging pain that seemed to be getting worse. He checked his watch. It was 6:05 AM. Opening day had already begun.

CHAPTER 25

S am awaited Opening Day in the North Woods Hunting
Area's parking lot. He sat in his cruiser and looked
over to the entrance for the trailhead that led to the North
Woods Hunting Area. Jake had guessed correctly. The
North Woods was the prime turkey area and would be Sam's
priority. He scanned the small parking lot and glanced down
at the heavily treed access road that led out to the main road.
No cars yet, he thought. Sam looked at his wristwatch. It was
0600 hours (6:00 AM). He nodded to himself, *Hunters
should have been here by now. Legal hours begin a half hour
before sunrise and that was at 0523. Where in hell are they?*.
Sam thought for a moment and raised his eyebrows. *Maybe
Lee's information leak on my patrol area for today got to more
hunters than we planned.*

It was just another Opening Day for another sport but
Sam felt uneasy. It wasn't Opening Day that bothered him.
It was the thought that Peg was at the cabin...and alone.
The boys had been shipped over to her parent's house for the
weekend. Traveller was with her and followed her around
the cabin until he became a necessary annoyance. Sam
wondered where Farmer was and what he was doing. He
was aware Farmer probably realized it was Opening Day for
turkey hunting and worried that he might consider that an
opportunity to harass the cabin again.

Sam felt his anxiety level begin to rise. *That bastard knows my territories and which ones I'm likely to cover. If he figures I'm working the favorite Opening Day area he might just head over to the cabin to harass Peg again.* Sam's thoughts began to get the best of him. *I hope this plan doesn't back fire on us.*

What if he sends some of his cabin people over there? Do I do the cautious thing and call for a replacement so I can go check on her? Then he realized Lee was right. Farmer's game was working. *Shit – Farmer has got me second guessing myself. Thompson P.D. has got two cruisers watching the cabin until I get home.* He immediately began to feel better. *I'm just going to follow through with the plan Lee and I discussed at his cabin… but I think I'll just give her a call before I head up the trail to the ravine.* He turned on his portable phone to dial and then turned it off. He murmured to himself, "She's probably up for the day now and pretty upset. If I call her now, she's going to demand I get back to the cabin. She's got the company of two cruisers, and Dispatch is on it. I'll let her calm a little and call when I get to the ravine. I know she can handle this."

Sam cursed to himself and then said aloud, "Let's go, Moody! Get it together. I have to get to the ravine so I can check these hunters coming in…don't want to spoil their hunt with a late arrival."

Sam pulled the mic from his car radio. "419, Headquarters."

Dispatch responded, "419, go."

"I'm at the North Woods Hunting Area. I'll be 44 for the next hour doing hunter safety checks."

Dispatch replied, "Roger 419. Call us on your portable for a wellbeing check from time to time."

Sam smiled, "Roger. 419 out."

— — —

The sun rose slowly over the East Hills. Peg Moody began to stir from her sleep. She opened her eyes to see the beautiful colors of a dawning day. The hills were still dark and peaceful. She reached across the bed to feel for Sam but he was gone. She knew he'd be on early patrol this morning but felt for him anyway. Traveller was asleep by her feet and raised one drowsy eye to meet her gaze. Then the conscious thoughts and memories of the last two weeks began to flood her mind. Famer's visit to the house, the rumors around town that came flooding through the telephone, and worst of all...her own imagination.

Peg sat up in bed with a start. *The kids...Oh yeah, the kids are at my mother's house for the weekend. A whole state away. Farmer doesn't even know who they are...they're safe there.* She looked back out the window and up into the hills. *Sam's up there. Why does he take these risks? Why?* She paused a moment as she became more lucid. *Well, at least Lee is up there with him. At least he's got someone watching over him.*

Peg turned and slipped her legs over the side of the bed when a frightening thought occurred to her. She was aware of the plan Sam and Lee had made but what if Farmer didn't take the bait. What if he hadn't heard the rumor Lee intentionally leaked about Sam's patrol area for today. What if he sent someone else to the North Woods Hunting Area...and comes here instead?

Peg knew how the criminal mind worked. She had plenty of experience with it when she worked as a probation officer and was usually level headed and reasonable. She raised her hands to her head and ran them through her hair, massaging her scalp as she did so. *I'm letting that creep get the best of me. I know I'm stronger than this. I'm better than this! I have to get some coffee and get a shower.* Then she remembered the cruisers and immediately began to relax. *Oh, that's right.*

Thompson P.D has got two cruisers watching the cabin. What am I worrying about? She smiled to herself and looked at Traveller, "Come on, boy. Let's go make some coffee." She grabbed her robe and headed downstairs to start the coffee pot. Traveller followed obediently.

The house was quiet...not usual for a Saturday morning at the Moody's cabin. The house felt cool and vacant, almost as if it was a dream. Peg got to the top of the stairs and slowly made her way down the pine stairway and finally into the kitchen. She turned on the water to fill the glass coffee pot and looked out the kitchen window toward the driveway. What she saw next caused her to drop the glass pot into the sink, where it broke into several pieces. Peg stepped back toward the kitchen wall with her hands at her mouth. Someone had spray painted the words DEAD MEAT, in red, across the entire window.

Peg stared at the window for a few minutes, then tried to calm herself. *Where are the cruisers? How did someone get past those cruisers to do this?* She looked out the front window adjacent to the driveway and saw one cruiser still parked at the far end of the driveway. She dropped her hands from her mouth and realized at least one cruiser was still there. *Someone must have got by the cops. Dark night, woods all around the cabin...who knows?* Peg, feeling as if she still had protection outside the cabin, collected herself and walked to the kitchen door that opened out onto the driveway and the side of the barn. Spray painted in big white letters against the side of the barn were the words, GOT YA. A crude smiley face was painted under the graffiti.

Traveller walked up to the kitchen door and pawed it while wagging his tail. Peg looked at him and thought, *He's got to go out. What do I do?* Cautiously, she forced herself to the door and opened it. Traveller took the opportunity and scrambled outside. Peg watched as Traveller poked around the yard. *If anyone was still out there, he'd know it by now. He's acting pretty normal, just his usual sniffing around. Everything seems to be okay.* Suddenly, Traveller raised his head as if someone had called him. He raised his nose high and seemed to be listening. He began wagging his tail and darting around the yard as if he was tracking an animal. He followed an invisible course around the yard which brought him to the tree line and finally back to the side of the house. The excited dog seemed very intent on some of the bushes near the house and under the front windows. Peg opened the door and looked down the driveway to see the policeman in his cruiser. He was watching her and waved when she stuck her head out the door.

"Traveller," She called. "Come on in, boy." Traveller stopped fussing with the bush under the picture window and obeyed. Peg looked back to the cruiser and motioned for the officer to come to the house. She closed the door and waited for the him to get to the kitchen door.

Finally, a wrinkled and tired looking cop stood on the farmer's porch outside the kitchen door. "Good morning, Mrs. Moody. Is everything alright?"

Peg tightened the robe around her neck and looked incredulously at the officer. "Well no, Officer. Sometime during the night someone must have come up to the house."

The officer seemed surprised, "What do you mean, Ma'am. I've been sitting here all night and Officer Simpson has been cruising the perimeter. Neither of us has seen any movement."

Peg explained what she had seen on the kitchen window and what was painted on the side of the barn. The officer went around the corner of the house and confirmed what Peg had described. He came back to the door where Peg stood.

"I don't understand, Mrs. Moody. We've been watching all night."

Peg motioned to where Traveller had been in the bushes. "Can you look behind those bushes please? My dog was sniffing around there quite a bit?"

The officer did so and then returned to where Peg stood. He took off his cap and scratched his head as he spoke. "I can't explain it, Ma'am. I found footprints under two of the windows…like someone was trying to look in the house." Peg raised her hands to her mouth.

The officer could see Peg was upset. "Ma'am, I saw Sam leave for patrol this morning at four AM. All of this had to have happened before he left for work. Sam wouldn't have noticed the spray paint because it was still dark. Obviously, someone got by us and vandalized the cabin, but if this was Farmer, at least you know he's not out there bothering Sam."

Peg heard what the officer said and began to relax a little. Then she looked back at the officer and said, "And what if it wasn't Farmer? What if it was one of his men?"

★★★★

CHAPTER 26

L ee Sparks travelled silently through the woods. The going was difficult in the darkness of the still sleeping forest. Use of the mag lite was out of the question as it was sure to tip off Farmer that he was being followed. Dawn was only minutes away as Lee reached the tree line at the south side of the North Woods Hunting Area. Visibility was a little better but he wasn't sure of Farmer's position yet. Any amount of darkness was welcome.

Lee approached the access road to the clearing and stopped just inside the tree line. The access road rose to a small incline making the clearing a little higher than the road. He scanned the area and saw Farmer's truck parked at the far end. Lee's eyes had adjusted to the darkness long ago allowing him to watch the truck without the use of his night vision binoculars. There was no movement in the truck.

He stepped out of the woods, and in a crouch, crept up the small incline. He watched the vehicle for a few minutes. *Looks vacant*, he thought. *I gotta' get after him if he's already left. I don't want him up on that ledge too long before I get there.*

Cautiously, Lee approached the truck, snuck up to the passenger side and peered into the front seat. He nodded his head. *He's gone.* Lee stood up and scanned the clearing and crept around to the driver's side. There were boot prints in the mud. He turned on his mag lite and saw they headed for the tree line to the rear of the truck. Lee saw the ragged opening in the trees. *He's climbing the old surveyor's cut line to the ridge.* Lee checked his watch. It was 5:45 AM. *He'll be up on that ridge in about thirty minutes.* Lee followed the boot prints to the cut line's opening. He knelt down and inspected the ground closely. Newly disturbed leaves showed their upturned sides and stood out from others that lay flat. Lee spoke softly to himself. "Yup he's gone through here." He looked up through the darkened cutline and although the morning was getting lighter, there was no sign of Farmer.

Lee followed the narrow cut line up a moderate slope. He constantly watched for signs that Farmer might have left. He knew Farmer must have been having difficulty with the climb because several branches and underbrush had been recently disturbed as if someone had stumbled. Finally, about half way up the old cutline, Lee saw something white on the ground. He smiled, *Farmer's getting sloppy.* He bent down and inspected the white tissue. *Blood*, Lee thought. He knelt down and turned on his mag lite. There was a large disturbance among the leaves as if someone had been rolling on the ground. Lee got down closer. One of the cut saplings showed blood on its cut end. He removed his glove and felt the end of the sharp shaft. The blood was still sticky. Lee looked closer. There was more blood on the sapling's shaft as well as on the leaves at its base. *He must have tripped and fallen onto one of these saplings and tried to stop the bleeding.* Lee looked up and tried to see through the roughly hacked corridor that led to the ridge. Still no sign of Farmer. *Well, he's hurt but it can't be too bad. He kept going.* More upturned leaves and broken branches became evident in the dawning light. Lee smiled, *I'm right behind him.*

— — —

Sam entered the trailhead that led to the ravine's hunting area. He began to feel comfortable about Peg's situation back at the cabin when suddenly his portable phone rang. It was Dispatch calling to report confirmed activity at Sam's cabin last night. The first thing Sam asked was if Peg was alright. Once Peg's welfare had been confirmed, Sam explained the footprints under the windows were probably his because he thought he had heard a noise by the side of the house as he was leaving for work. It was dark and the trees that encircled the cabin made it seem darker with their shadows. He couldn't see much but had gone back to the house to investigate. Sam went on to explain that he checked behind the bushes and tested some of the windows to ensure they were locked. That explained why Traveller had stopped his furious tracking around the yard and went to the bushes wagging his tail. He had recognized Sam's scent. However, there was still concern about the graffiti on the window and on the barn. Someone must have gotten by the police guard.

Dispatch asked if he wanted to be relieved from patrol. Sam declined and said he'd call Peg to check on her wellbeing. Dispatch acknowledged and Sam turned off his phone.

★★★★

CHAPTER 27

Marine Sergeant Tom Stafford was just beginning his day at the Thompson Police Department. He had decided to come in a little early to get some paperwork done in lieu of the upcoming boating season. Marine patrol schedules and maintenance records all needed attention. Tom stepped out of his car and looked east at the dawning sky. The sun had not yet risen from behind the East Hills. He stopped to watch the sun come up but it would be a while yet. Dawn was at its transition from night to day and the moon still floated in the sky. It was a beautiful sight. One that the observer wished someone else was around to share with. It was dark but still light which emphasized the deep purples and lighter blues of the impending dawn.

Tom took a deep breath of cool spring air. *Ah, it'll be a while yet. Better get in there and get started.* He scanned the hills to the north and reminded himself. *I love springtime. Everything coming out new, trees beginning to bud, flowers blossoming…snow finally gone.* Then it hit him. *Hey, It's Opening Day for turkey hunting! I wonder where Sam is patrolling today.*

Tom scanned his ID card at the door and walked through the officer's entrance. He started for the cafeteria to get a quick coffee before going to the locker room. Lieutenant Alban had the same idea and came around the corner almost colliding with him. Tom stopped short to avoid the lieutenant. "Good morning, LT."

Alban nodded back at Tom and smiled. "Good morning, Tom. Come on. Let me buy you a coffee."

The two wardens walked to the coffee machine with Alban in the lead. Alban was unusually quiet so Tom struck up a conversation. "Hey, LT. It's Opening Day for turkey… spring is finally here."

Alban grumbled and murmured something Tom didn't understand. When Tom didn't reply, Alban motioned to a table and the two officers sat down. An awkward silence ensued as Alban looked into his coffee. Suddenly, and without lifting his gaze from the table, Alban commented on Tom's statement. "Another Opening Day. More guys running around in the woods with guns and knives… Oh, boy."

Tom looked at the lieutenant and thought, *Boy, he's in a great mood.* "Well that reminds me, LT. I've heard the stories about Farmer out of prison and the harassment at Sam's cabin. Where is Sam's patrol today? Does he have a partner?"

Alban snapped his head quickly toward Tom as if he hadn't considered the situation. "Sam set up the patrols for Opening Day. Now that you mention it, he never said a word about where he was going or who he was taking with him."

Tom rolled his eyes and thought, *Here we go again.*

Alban stood from the table. "I'm thinking he probably took his buddy, Pat James. You're busy with marine duty so it's obvious he wouldn't have asked you." Alban put his coffee cup down hard on the table as he stared into Tom's face. "Ah shit! I hope he didn't go out on his own hoping to bump into Farmer." Tom said nothing, but in his mind knew that was exactly what Sam had done. Alban left in a rush,

"Thanks, Tom. I gotta' go check the duty roster. Meanwhile, get what you need from your locker and get up to the North Woods Hunting Area. If Sam is on his way into the ravine, you'll need to take a shortcut. Take the old logging road near Sam's cabin. It dumps out onto the hunter's parking lot for the North Woods area."

Tom rose from the table with a start. Alban was already leaving the room but shouted back over his shoulder as he passed through the door. "Get going! Code two. No siren - lights only." Alban disappeared into the adjoining hallway.

Tom ran to the nearest desk phone and called Peg. The phone rang and rang. Tom became more anxious as the moments passed. He had to get to the North Woods Hunting Area. "Come on Peg, answer the phone," he murmured.

Finally, Peg picked up. "Hello?"

Tom was almost demanding. "Peg, It's Tom Stafford. Do you happen to know who Sam took with him on patrol this morning?" Peg hesitated and Tom picked up on it. He continued, "Peg it's very important. We think he's out looking for Farmer. Come clean with me if you know."

Peg thought for a moment and considered what could go wrong. "Okay, okay. Sam is the only warden up in the North Woods. Lee Sparks is kind of with him."

Tom felt a rush of frustration run through his entire body. "Peg…Come on. Spill it. What do you mean, …kind of?"

Peg knew Tom was in Sam's corner so she explained their plan to lure Farmer into the North Woods Hunting Area. Tom shook his head from side to side as he listened. "Okay Peg, thanks. I gotta' move." Tom slammed the phone back down in its cradle.

★★★★

CHAPTER 28

D awn began to break quickly, melting away the greys and purples of the cool morning. The sun finally cleared the top of the east hills and began to brighten the valley. Jake Farmer sat on the ridge with his back against the table rock he planned to use as his shooting platform. He reached over to his day pack and pulled it close. He unzipped the main pouch and reached inside to find the one bullet cartridge he brought along for his mission. Finally, he had it in his fingers and pulled it from the pack. He raised the bullet to his face and stared at it for a moment.

The little piece of lead and powder was going to make everything equal. In his own distorted mind, the use of one little bullet was going to make amends for the years of antagonizing torture Sam Moody had caused him. It would remove the source of all his bitterness and guilt Moody had unknowingly placed upon him. It would be payback for all the trouble Moody had caused between Jake and the Fish and Game Department as well as the Police Department. It would be payback for ruining his thirty-five-year career as a state game warden and ruining his reputation. Jake now realized Moody was responsible for everything that had gone wrong in his life. That goody two-shoes academy puke was going to pay.

Jake began to think back and remembered how Moody had made it his business to follow him all the way up to New

Hampshire just to harass him. That action had caused him a heart attack and near paralysis. He remembered Moody coming out of the dark that night in the New Hampshire field and tackling him and how they wrestled in the tall hay grass. Jake thought, *That was so far out of his jurisdiction, and what do they do…make him a sergeant.* Jake's blood pressure began to rise as he thought of all the months that caused him. Forced to lie motionless in some stuffy old hospital, day after day, getting poked and prodded by nurses and doctors, only to have prison waiting for him when he was healthy enough to leave. *That sonuvabitch,* he thought. *And then he brings that bitch Helen Woodruff to see me so she can give me another heart attack.* Jake thought about that for a moment too. *I bet they got together and planned that whole thing. They knew I couldn't move and Helen kept threatening to turn my oxygen off. Just scaring me…making my blood pressure go higher and higher…that bitch. Girlfriend my ass! I'm gonna' get her too.*

Jake took the cartridge and slid it into the rifle's loading chamber. *Better get ready, Moody ought to be coming down that path any minute.* Jake turned around so he was leaning against the table rock. He adjusted his position so his chest was against the rock and his legs were half bent and comfortably placed behind him, his right leg lying on top of his left.

Jake reached up and focused his rifle scope on a tree Sam would have to pass by as he entered the clearing. He reached up and adjusted his scope and put his cross hairs on the center of the same tree. *Moody has got to pass right in front of that birch tree…should be within two feet. When his head covers that tree trunk, I'll shoot. Distance is about fifty yards and I'm about a hundred feet above him.* Jake adjusted the scope for the vertical angle.

— — —

Minutes passed and Jake kept his rifle fixed on the birch tree at the opening of the trailhead to the ravine. His side began to ache causing him to waver. He began to perspire and the sweat was travelling down his forehead into his eyes. Slowly Jake moved his right hand away from the rifle's trigger while supporting the gun with his left. Jake was getting impatient. *Where is that sonuvabitch?* He checked his watch. It was almost 6:30. He reached into his breast pocket and pulled out a cloth to wipe his brow. Finishing the task, he dropped the cloth onto the rock and cautiously brought his hand back to the firing position.

Finally, there was movement among the trees at the trailhead. Sam Moody stepped out of the trees and stopped at the trailhead's entrance to the ravine. Jake moved the lever action of the .30-30 rifle slowly, gently transferring the bullet into the firing chamber. He held his firing position supported by the flat rock for several minutes. Sam just stood there looking into the ravine. Jake grew impatient. *What's he doing? Why doesn't he move forward?* The minutes felt like hours. Jake made a slight body adjustment while holding the rifle in the same position, and watched Sam through the scope. He spoke quietly to himself, "Come on Sammy boy…two more steps."

★★★★

CHAPTER 29

The sun was coming strong and bright. Sam looked up and southeast from the trailhead. *Man that's bright for mid-May*, he thought.

Suddenly his portable radio crackled to life. "Headquarters to 419."

Sam stepped back a few steps into the shade and pulled his radio from its holster. "At the trailhead to the North Woods ravine."

Dispatch continued, "419 there seems to be some confusion on patrol assignments. LT is asking who is with you."

Sam dropped the radio to waist level and looked up into the branches that shaded him from the morning sun. *Damn it. If Alban finds out I'm alone he's going to want to send me a partner. He doesn't know Lee is up here with me and has no idea we're trying to lure Farmer into a trap. He could blow the whole plan right now.* Sam keyed his radio, "419/ Dispatch. Reception is poor in this area. I repeat. I am at the trailhead to the North Woods ravine. I'll call in on my portable phone as soon as is convenient." Sam smiled to himself and thought, *They know I'm here to check hunters. That transmission ought to buy me some time. As far as they know I could be in the middle of a hunter safety check.*

Lieutenant Alban stood behind the dispatcher and heard Sam's reply. "Damn Moody! He's by himself."

Cautiously, the dispatcher asked, "Do you want me to send another warden to meet up with Sam, LT?"

Alban thought for a moment then replied. "No,… thanks. Wait for Moody's phone call. I'm stretched pretty thin on personnel assignments today because of Opening Day. That may be why he's alone." Alban turned and left Dispatch slamming the door behind him.

— — —

Up on the ridge Lee came out of the tree line in time to see Farmer sighting in on a target. Lee felt a rush of adrenalin travel up his spine. *Damn, I hope that's not Sam he's targeting.* Lee couldn't tell if Farmer was only sighting in, or about to shoot. *Damn it, he's about 200 feet from me. Either I take a shot now or gamble and try to get close as quick as I can. Can't take the chance he's shooting at Sam or just trying to scare him.*

Lee threw down his pack and unslung his.300 mag rifle from his shoulder as he broke into a run. Luckily the ridge top was hard, flat rock and was suitable for running. Lee was getting closer and there was no rifle shot yet. He stopped to assess the situation and saw Farmer work the action of his rifle. He had sighted in on his target and was now transferring the bullet into the firing chamber. Lee's heart began to race. *No time. He's gonna' shoot.* Lee had to do something fast. Stealth was no longer an option. The only thing Lee could do was shout. "**FARMER!**"

— — —

Sam waited a few minutes at the trailhead and waited for more radio transmissions. The radio remained quiet.

Okay, no calls. They think I'm busy. Let's get on with this. Sam stepped out into the sunshine and stopped again to put on his sunglasses.

Farmer had his crosshairs locked on Sam's forehead. The sudden shout from Lee came just as he pulled the trigger.

— — —

Tom Stafford was out of breath. He had arrived at the North Woods Hunting Area in record time. He grabbed his rifle, jumped from the patrol Blazer, and let the door slam behind him as he raced down the trail toward the ravine. Tom ran as fast as he could. He looked up ahead and saw the opening to the ravine …and Sam standing in front of it. Tom stopped and looked up through the forest canopy and saw the ledge's rim. There was a reflection with what appeared to be a human head behind it. Tom felt a rush of adrenalin. *Rifle scope! Farmer!* Out of breath, Tom tried to shout but his voice wouldn't carry.

There was a sharp rifle crack and Sam went down in a heap. He fell backward, unconscious and bleeding from the head. Blood from a wound over his left eye oozed as life nutrients exited in wide, bright red pulses. Sam Moody lay motionless on the soft earth of the trailhead's path. His world was now dark and quiet.

Stafford raised his own rifle, sighted on the assassin, took a breath and a half, and squeezed the trigger.

★★★★

CHAPTER 30

L ee heard the rifle shot and went to a kneeling position to shoot. As he raised his.300 mag to the firing position, he heard another rifle shot. He watched in surprise as Farmer's head jerked back suddenly. His entire body seemed to go rigid, for only a second. Then, as if in slow motion, he appeared to go limp and slowly rolled back onto the table rock. The rifle fell to the side. Jake Farmer was dead.

Lee stood from his kneeling position in utter surprise. *Sam couldn't have made that shot with his.357 revolver, even if he saw Farmer.* Lee knew Farmer was out of range and Sam wasn't carrying a rifle.

Lee walked the few yards to Farmer's body. It lay sprawled across the table rock he had used for a shooting platform. There was a pool of blood spreading across the rock from under Farmer's left arm and near his head by the mouth. Lee stepped a little closer and nudged Farmer with his boot. No reaction. It looked as if the bullet came from somewhere below, near the entrance to the ravine. The vertical angle caused the bullet to enter under Farmer's left arm which held the rifle and probably travelled upward or across into his lungs. The head seemed unharmed.

Lee bent over the dead body and felt for the carotid artery. No pulse. As Lee began to straighten up, he glanced down into the ravine to see Sam lying motionless at the trailhead. A feeling of panic ran through Lee's entire body as he shouted into the Ravine, **"NOooo…..!"**

Lee began to make for the edge of the ravine in an effort to start down when he saw a uniformed officer appear at the trailhead. He spoke aloud, "Who could that be?" He grabbed his binoculars from his front pocket and focused on the two men on the floor of the ravine. "Tom Stafford! Thank God! But how…" Lee shouted to Tom from his position on the ledge and waved his arms.

Tom heard someone shout from above and spun around. In one graceful motion, he chambered another round and brought his rifle to his shoulder in preparation to shoot. He looked up and recognized a distraught Lee Sparks waving to him from the ridge above. Tom waved him down as he checked over Sam's bleeding head.

★★★★

CHAPTER 31

L ee stumbled and tripped in an uncoordinated fashion as he tried to descend the steep slope. Once on the ravine floor he ran the last hundred feet to where Sam lay and stopped short. Stafford was working on a wound to Sam's forehead. "Is he alive?"

Stafford answered without looking up. "Yeah, so far. Looks like the bullet grazed the left side of his forehead, right above the temple. He's probably got a bad concussion to boot." Tom turned his head up to meet Lee's concerned face. "What about the shooter?"

Lee replied as he stared at his fallen friend. "Dead. It was Jake Farmer."

Tom said nothing then turned his attention back to Sam and finished wrapping his head with part of his undershirt to slow the bleeding. "Lee, hold his head while I call in for a medevac." Lee knelt down by Sam and held his head with both hands. Tom stood up and pulled his portable radio from its holster. "Headquarters from 422. Shots fired... Shots fired. Officer down, one other has expired. North Woods hunting area. Require a medevac ASAP."

Dispatch replied, "Roger 422. Officer down, another expired, North Woods hunting area. Medevac alerted. Provide personal injuries."

Tom looked back down at the unconscious Sam. "Rifle shot to the forehead above the left eye. Appears to be a grazing blow. Severe concussion probable. Other casualty is a civilian and has expired."

Dispatch acknowledged, "422, Chopper is airborne and enroute to your location. ETA is ten minutes."

★★★★

CHAPTER 32

S am Lay unconscious in a hospital bed. He had slept through the helicopter ride and transfer to Hilltown General Hospital. A team of doctor's had just finished examining the bullet wound and were quietly discussing their opinions at the back of his room. Peg, Lee and Tom Stafford sat in a patient lounge area awaiting the doctor's prognosis on Sam.

Peg sat holding her head with both hands and stared at the floor, unable to hold a complete conversation. She blamed herself for knowing what the plan was and allowing Sam to go forth with what she considered using him as human bait. Tom Stafford sat by her side and held her hand. Lee Sparks stood by the lounge window and stared out into the openness. No one spoke but each of them searched their brains for something or someone they could blame. Each of them had their own explanation for why Sam was in the condition he was but no one considered why they had been put in a position to act as they did.

The hours passed. Finally, Pat James, one of Sam's best friends and fellow warden, burst through the lounge doors. His huge frame seemed to fill the entire double doorway. He carried a bouquet of flowers in his right hand and gently passed them to Peg. Pat bent over and kissed her on the cheek. "Peg, I'm so sorry. I was involved with an arrest that went bad in the West Hills Territory and have been tied up at the county jail for hours. Dispatch called me when they were airlifting Sam from the ravine. I came as soon as I could."

Pat's apology only caused Peg to begin sobbing again. She didn't even look up at the concerned warden. Pat knelt down in front of her and tried to qualify his absence. "Peg, he never mentioned anything to me about what he was doing up there in the North Woods. If he had, I would have been there. Considering everything we've been through together…and he never said a word." She nodded and patted his hand. Tom took the flowers from Peg and went to find a vase.

Presently the hallway doors opened and one of Sam's doctors approached the apprehensive group. The name tag on his white robe said Doctor Charles, Chief of Neuro Surgery. Everyone stood up and turned to meet the approaching doctor. Lee turned from the window but stayed where he was. The doctor remained stoic. There was no way to read what he was about to say. No way to get information any faster.

Doctor Charles stopped in front of the worried group. He tucked his clipboard between his chest and folded arms. "Good afternoon, folks. I'll get to the point as quickly as I can. The bullet grazed the frontal bone above Sam's left eye. There was no penetration to the skull although the skull was creased by the bullet." Peg wavered a bit but Tom caught her under both arms and held her up. Doctor Charles paused until Peg seemed steady. "The rifle found as the apparent weapon was a.30-30." The doctor paused and looked at the group. "The caliber of a bullet from that rifle carries a huge impact force, and in this case, only part of that force was transferred to Sam's head. The crease in his skull will heal in time and he'll carry a three-inch scar from now on." The doctor paused for a moment to let the group digest the information, then continued. "Eventually, he'll return to normal. He's going to have some pretty big headaches for a while but we'll give him some meds for that."

The whole room seemed to relax. Doctor Charles finally smiled, "Any questions?" Peg managed to ask, "Will there be any long term affects? I mean any problems with the way his brain may have been affected or his motor skills."

Doctor Charles shrugged his shoulders. "Not from what the Electroencephalogram scans say. He'll probably have some blurred vision for a while but that too should subside with time." The doctor paused and added, "I mean… anything can happen, but from what we can see now, he should be able to resume as normal in a few weeks. I'm suggesting a two-month medical leave of absence."

Peg was relieved and exhausted at the same time. She dropped into the nearest lounge chair and let her head rest against its high back with her eyes closed. She thought about nothing. Her mind was blank…empty. She needed sleep.

★★★★

CHAPTER 33

Two days passed and Sam finally began to stir from his comatose state. The doctors had placed him in a medically induced coma as a precaution to swelling of the brain and other scenarios that could arise. A nurse stood by his bed reading the charts and looked down to see Sam begin to regain consciousness. Peg sat on the other side of the bed holding his hand. "Mrs. Moody. Sam is beginning to come out of it. Greet him back gently and slowly. Be soothing…and smile."

Sam's eyes fluttered at first and then it appeared as if he was trying to clear them after a long sleep. His eyebrows began to move around and finally his eyes were open. He looked drowsy but stared straight ahead as if there was no one else in the room. Peg squeezed his hand gently and murmured, "Hey, Sam. I'm right here. Can you hear me?"

The voice seemed so far away – so distant. Sam heard her and slowly turned his head in her direction. He could see Peg leaning toward him, holding his hand with both of hers. She appeared blurry at first but became more distinct as he tried to focus. Her long, brown hair drooped to the bed and her bangs were askew in front of her eyes. The big brown eyes he had always adored…the same ones that seemed to light up when she was angry, and the same ones that could be so soft in a loving moment, locked with his own. It was the most comforting feeling he'd ever experienced.

He smiled and squeezed her hand. It was Peg. She was here and she was safe. What had happened? He wondered where he was and how he got here. He wasn't in any pain but felt extremely tired. He began to say something and Peg put a finger up to his lips. "Don't talk yet. Just look at me." Sam complied and just looked into Peg's eyes. "Everything is okay and you'll be out of here soon. The boys can't wait to see you and your brother Cyrus is out in the waiting room with Tom and Pat. Lee has been here since they brought you in.

Peg continued to lean forward on Sam's bed, resting her left forearm on his left thigh and gently stroked his brown hair with her right hand. Sam closed his eyes as Peg whispered soft words to him that only he could hear.

"He's asleep, Mrs. Moody. He is out of the coma now, but sleeping it off…so to speak. He'll be in and out of these little cat naps for a day or so. It's all very normal and he's doing well. I suggest you go home and take Sam's pals with you. He won't be up for any visitors for another day."

Peg looked at the nurse and stroked Sam's hair one more time. She bent over and kissed him the cheek and whispered something in his ear. Then she stood, thanked the nurse and left the room.

— — —

Tom, Pat, Cyrus and Lee stood in the middle of the patient lounge quietly discussing the situation when they saw Peg come through the double doors. The four friends stopped talking as Peg approached. "Cyrus, take me home. I want to call my boys." The four looked at each other.

Pat gently asked, "Peg, is he going to be okay? Will he be here long?" Peg stopped and looked at the group.

"Oh, I'm sorry. I'm just tired and cranky." She dropped into the nearest lounge chair and the four anxious friends sat or knelt next to her. "Sam just woke from the coma. He looked at me and was going to say something but looked very tired. He fell back to sleep and won't be ready for visitors for twenty-four hours."

The four men brightened. Tom was the first to speak as he grabbed her left arm. "Peg that is great news! What a relief!"

Peg put her hand up to stop Tom short. "The doctor had a chance to speak to me before Sam woke up. From the information they received from the site investigation team, Sam was really, really lucky. The distance and angle of trajectory was all reconfigured and it appears the shot should have killed Sam." She paused a moment then continued, "They looked at his boot prints before he fell and it looks as if he stopped to do something right before the shooting. Dispatch reports they spoke to him on his portable radio at 6:30 AM. Then there was another set of his boot prints together indicating he took a couple more steps and stopped again. Those were found at his feet when Tom found him, indicating he fell backward after the shot." The four men looked at each other confused.

Pat spoke up. "Peg, He's okay…the bullet missed…he's going to be okay." Peg shook her head and replied.

"You don't understand. He apparently stopped right in line with the shooter's planned trajectory. His sunglasses were found lying on the ground a few feet to the left of his head. They think he stopped before going out into the ravine to put on his sunglasses and when he tipped his head to put them on is what saved his life. That's why the bullet only grazed his skull. Otherwise it would have hit him square in the center of his forehead. He would be dead right now if not for that." Peg started crying again. "I just can't get my head around that."

Lee reached forward and put his hand on Peg's right arm. "But it only grazed him, Peg. He's alive."

Peg looked up and glared at Lee. She shook his hand from her arm violently. "…And…where were you? You were supposed to be watching for Farmer."

Lee's mouth dropped open in surprise. He stood from his kneeling position. The others remained quiet.

"Peg, I was too far from Farmer and only had enough time to shout his name when I saw he was going to take the shot. I didn't even know what he was shooting at."

Tom interjected, "Peg, Lee's sudden shout was probably enough of a distraction to throw Farmer's aim off. Remember, Farmer knew he was about to commit a murder. A sudden surprise from behind would have disturbed his concentration enough to throw his aim off."

Peg stood from her seated position. She looked away from Lee and glanced at Tom. She glared at Lee one more time and left the lounge. Lee walked back to the window. It was clear he wanted to be alone.

Cyrus started after Peg and nodded at the group as he left and glanced at Tom and Pat as he went by. "Watch Lee. Walk out with him. Don't say anything unless he says something to you first." The two wardens nodded and sat back down and waited. They knew it would be a while before the wily tracker decided it was time to go.

★★★★

CHAPTER 34

Lieutenant Gene Alban knocked on Fish and Game Captain John Fletcher's office door. There was the usual pause then a loud but Curt "Come," came from within. Alban walked through the door and Fletcher motioned for him to take a seat in front of his desk. Fletcher said nothing as he watched Alban approach. The aging captain was totally unreadable.

Alban took his seat and sat bolt upright in his chair. The captain paused for a moment as if he was trying to read what showed on the lieutenant's face. "Well, how is Sam? Is he going to make it?" Alban remained a little apprehensive. He was still unsure of why Fletcher had called him in.

"Sam has come out of the coma and was listening to his wife as she welcomed him back. She also told me he was about to say something but she stopped him. As of this moment, he has been drifting in and out of consciousness which the hospital says is normal…especially after an induced coma."

Fletcher sat back in his big office chair and nodded his head as if to indicate he was satisfied with Alban's report about Sam. He fussed about his middle desk drawer an pulled out his pipe, tapped it a few times on the side of his desk and started packing tobacco into it.

Alban began to offer a statement. "Cap, I...," but Fletcher stifled whatever Alban was going to say with a raised hand in a halting fashion. Alban remained quiet and watched the captain prepare to light his pipe.

Fletcher took a few puffs from the old corncob pipe and blew the smoke into the air above Alban's head. "Okay Lieutenant, why was Sam up in that area alone on Opening Day considering the impending threat from Jake Farmer, and why was he even on duty? He should have been home until the whole Farmer thing blew over. Hell, I have reports from the cops and Dispatch that someone actually penetrated our police line around the Moody property the night before." Fletcher blew another puff of smoke over Alban's head.

Alban replied calmly, "Sir, Sergeant Moody was in charge of patrol assignments for Opening Day. I didn't even think to question what he was doing, let alone assume he might be going up into the North Woods by himself." Fletcher slammed his right hand down on the desk hard. "Gene! You, as well as everyone else knew Farmer was a threat because of his visitations to the Moody residence. Shit! Didn't you read Sam at that meeting we had with the state judicial people?" Fletcher paused as he glared at Alban. "You know...the one about Farmer stalking the Moody property!"

Alban tried to interject a comment. "Yes sir, but..."

Fletcher cut him off. "It was obvious Sam saw right through the red tape...all that constitutional rights bullshit. He came right out and said that if he felt Famer was a threat to his family he wouldn't hesitate to react. Didn't that clue you in that he might be thinking about planning some kind of retaliation? Sam had the perfect set up with Opening Day right around the corner."

Alban remained quiet for a moment then began, "Captain, I know Sam. He is not one to scare easily. To answer your question…yes, I did hear what he said but I didn't take it as a threat. Sam tends to sit back and watch a situation before he takes action."

Captain Fletcher stood from his desk and began walking about the room. "The Site Investigation Team did a study around the area of Farmer's body. It seems they found another set of boot prints found in the sand on that ledge. The age of the prints coincides with the time of the shooting." Alban appeared shocked. Fletcher turned around and raised his voice. "Those same boot prints match a pair of boot prints… military style…found near Sam. In fact, those same prints were found near Sam's head with slight depressions in the dirt path…like the boot's owner had kneeled by his head." Fletcher took a moment to calm down and resumed pacing the room puffing furiously on his pipe.

Alban stood from his chair. "Are you implying that Sam may have planned something but it backfired?"

Fletcher stopped pacing and turned to look at the confused lieutenant. Now calmer, Fletcher replied. "Gene, I'm surprised you missed this. You say you know Sam. Hell, I know Sam and I know he's not someone to mess with, especially when it comes to his family." Fletcher paused and tapped his pipe on the side of his desk. "I think Sam was up there by himself because he knew he had back up from someone…not from the department either. I spoke with the Site Investigation Team leader and he said that should have been an easy shot from that distance with the scope that was on Farmer's rifle." Fletcher sat back down. "So, how did he miss?"

Alban began with Tom Stafford's account. "Stafford said he saw Sam standing at the trailhead opening just before he heard the shot and…"

Fletcher cut him off again. "I know all about putting on the sunglasses, etcetera, etcetera. There had to be some other distraction…there had to be something else. Farmer was an expert with a rifle."

Now, Alban paced the large office floor. "Well, Sir. You may be right but we have no witnesses. Farmer is dead and Sergeant Stafford arrived just as the shot was fired. I understand there are another set of fresh boot prints but a lot of hunters use that style. They're not Stafford's so where do we go from there? We can't check everyone's boots. That's a heavily hunted area."

Fletcher looked up at Alban with disbelief. "Gene. You just said it. Stafford was there just before the rifle shot, then he shot the shooter…thinking it was probably Farmer. Then Sam was down. There wasn't enough time for a third party to get to Sam without Stafford seeing him."

★★★★

CHAPTER 35

Tom Stafford sat in front of his television watching but not seeing anything on the screen. His mind kept drifting back to Sam lying in the hospital, and of Peg and their sons. *That bastard Farmer*, he thought. *The guy was so warped he probably thought his revenge was justified.* Suddenly the phone rang shaking Tom from his deep thoughts.

"Stafford, here."

There was a momentary pause on the phone and Lieutenant Alban's voice came through the receiver. "Tom –Lieutenant Alban. The Captain and I need to see you down here pronto."

Tom replied, "Uh Okay, LT. Like, right now?"

Alban came back quick. "Right now, Tom. Get in your car and get down here ASAP. Meet me in Fletcher's office."

Tom agreed and hung up the phone and thought. *Now what? They pulled me in on this North Woods mess and now I have to go before the Captain.*

— — —

Tom Stafford sat in front Captain Fletcher's desk. Fletcher sat behind the desk and Alban stood by the book shelf to Fletcher's right. Fletcher waited for Tom to get comfortable as he re-read Tom's accounting of what he had reported on the North Woods shooting incident. The room was quiet. Alban stared at the floor.

Finally, Fletcher glanced up at Tom and slid his eyeglasses down his nose with a quick move of his left hand. "Thanks for coming in, Mr. Stafford."

Tom nodded, "Absolutely, Sir."

The Captain looked back down at the report. "Tom, your report only mentions yourself and Sam in the ravine when Sam was shot." Fletcher stopped and looked up at Tom again. "Is there anything else you want to add to this?"

Tom stared right into Fletcher's eyes. "What do you mean, Cap?"

Fletcher slammed his hand down on the desk. "Damn it, Tom! If you falsify anything on this report, it could mean your job or even prison! I suggest you come clean this instant!"

Marine Sergeant Tom Stafford sat back in his chair and took a deep breath before speaking. "Captain, I knew nothing of what led up to this entire show except that Sergeant Moody was being harassed by Jake Farmer since Farmer's release from prison. Sam never even discussed it with me. I was on my way into work when the LT invited me for a cup of coffee. During that conversation the LT realized Sam may have been alone up in the North Woods hunting area and told me he might need me to go there in the next few minutes…which is what I did. The rest of it is in that report."

Fletcher leaned across the desk. "Sergeant Stafford you are one of my best wardens. I know you are honest and trust worthy but I need to know if there may have been someone else in that ravine after Sam was shot."

Tom was still staring into the Captain's eyes. *It sounds like they know there was someone else in the area at the time of the shooting. If I try to cover this up, we're all going down. I better just tell what I know.*

"Well, Sir. There was an individual who appeared to come from the area where the shot was fired and lent a hand in tending to Sam's wounds. It was obvious he had nothing to do with the shooting and stayed until the chopper took Sam away.

Fletcher looked at Alban and nodded. "Do you know his name Mr. Stafford?"

Tom thought fast, *They haven't identified him yet. They probably found the other set of boot prints and know there was someone else. I'll be vague.* "He's a professional tracker and outdoor guide that lives in the hills...kind of a recluse. I think Sam knows him...name is Lee. From what I know, he keeps to himself. It looked like he had been hunting, heard the shot, and came to see what happened. I didn't notice him until after I started working on Sam and looked up toward the ravine's ledge. He was waving frantically at me and shouting something I couldn't understand."

Fletcher was staring hard into Tom's eyes. Fletcher asked, "Lee what? What is his last name?" Tom dropped his gaze to the floor. Fletcher continued, "Mr. Stafford!."

Tom replied with his head down. "Sparks...Lee Sparks."

Fletched continued to press Tom. "Do you think we can find him to ask him what he saw?"

Tom remained calm, "I know he works the hills, Cap but I don't know exactly where he lives. I can keep my eyes open for him but he isn't a suspect, is he?"

Fletcher grimaced. *Smart guy. He knows the guy isn't a suspect in the shooting...just more detail for us.* Fletcher replied in a soft fatherly tone. "Tom, Ballistics confirmed the bullet pulled from that birch tree was from Farmer's rifle, and

Farmer who had a motive is dead. If there was another witness I want to know what he saw."

Fletcher stood up from his desk. "You are dismissed Sergeant and you are on report. In the future, please note any and all people that may have been in the area, suspicious or not, will be included in your investigation.

Tom stood to leave and Fletcher added one last item. "Sergeant Stafford, I want Lee Sparks in here for questioning. Tell him he is not a suspect. I just want to know what he might have seen. One of our wardens was ambushed and I mean to find out if there is any more to it. Is that understood?"

Tom faced the Captain before turning away. "Yes, Sir."

Fletcher looked back down at his desk, "Dismissed."

★★★★

CHAPTER 36

Four days had pass ed and Peg called Tom Stafford to let him know Sam was able to see visitors. She caught the sullen warden at his desk writing shift assignments for marine patrols in the next few weeks. Tom picked up the desk phone. "Marine Department. Sergeant Stafford speaking."

The voice that came through the receiver was upbeat and cheery. "Hi Tom, It's Peg Moody."

Tom dropped his paperwork and picked up his pen. "Hey Peg, how's our boy?"

Peg replied, "He's allowed visitors and making improvements each day. He told me to tell you and Pat to get in there."

A chill ran up Tom's spine. The realization he was going to have to confront Sam with the idea he had reported Lee's presence during the shooting incident had been causing him to lose sleep. The worst part was that he was going to have to bring Lee in for questioning. "Oh okay, Peg. Tell Sam I'll be there tonight after dinner. I'll be alone. Pat has graveyard tonight, but I'll let him know." Tom lied. Pat really didn't have a late shift that night but he didn't want Pat to hear him explain how he had provided the Fish and Game brass with Lee's presence in the ravine.

Peg heard something unusual in Tom's voice and her smile faded. "Okay, Tom. I'll tell him."

Tom hung up the desk phone. He gazed out his office window and thought about what he was going to have do. *I guess tonight's the night I let Sam know what happened and I've got to get a map from him that will take me to Lee's cabin. No one's ever been up there except Sam, and when I do get up there, I'm going to have to tell him I have to take Lee in for questioning. Shit! Can it get any worse?*

— — —

Sam Moody sat propped up in his hospital bed glaring at Tom Stafford. "I can't believe you told Alban and Fletcher about Lee. What were you thinking?"

Tom stood at the foot of Sam's bed feeling as if he was a snitch. "Sam! You and Lee kept me out of this whole thing. I didn't know anything about it until I went to work that morning and asked Alban who was with you. I didn't know about any...plan, so how was I supposed to know what or what not say?" Tom shook his head and walked over to the window to lean against the wall.

The room was quiet for a few minutes, then Sam asked in a calmer tone, "How did you find out about our plan?"

Tom stared at Sam for a moment, *Now I'm going to be getting Peg into trouble.* Finally, Tom blurted it out. "Look, Sam. I don't know what you guys were thinking but the plan turned to shit and you almost died." Stafford walked back toward Sam's bed. He leaned forward to emphasize the point. "Do you understand? You were almost killed!" Tom paused, "Doesn't that mean anything to you? Almost killed... and you're worried about Lee Sparks! I got there just before Farmer pulled the trigger. You were damn lucky." Sam started to say something about how Lee may have distracted the shooter by shouting at him but Tom cut him off. "Yeah, yeah.

Well, thank God for Lee." Tom began to walk away from the bed and turned around to face Sam again. "Tell me…what were you going to do if Lee had caught Farmer in time?"

Sam took a deep breath and began to explain. "The plan was to catch Farmer in the act. We had to get proof that Farmer was on a vendetta against me and my family, so we had to play it close. We had planned it so Lee would be right on his tail, watch him set up and as soon as he sighted on me, thwart the whole situation."

Tom threw a towel across the room. "And what was he going to do…shoot him? The whole thing borders on entrapment, Sam."

Sam sat bolt upright in bed. "We did not entrap the sonuvabitch. We merely leaked info on my patrol area for that morning in the hope Farmer would pick up on it. We didn't lure him in at all."

Tom rubbed his forehead as if giving up on the conversation. "Okay, look pal. I've got to go up into the High Meadow and bring Lee back for questioning. Fletcher said he's not a suspect but needs to know what else…if anything, he may have seen. So, I need a map to Lee's cabin."

Sam frowned and asked for a paper and pen. When Sam finished the map, he handed it back to Tom over the bed's portable table. "Be careful up there. Lee knows I'm the only one that knows his whereabouts. He'll probably see you coming well in advance." Tom took the map and nodded his head. As Tom turned to leave the room, Sam stopped him. "Tom, they told me what you did for me up there. I mean besides shooting Farmer…the bandaging, calling in the medevac…Thanks." Tom managed a weak smile, nodded his head and left the room.

★★★★

CHAPTER 37

The hike up into the High Meadow region of Thompson was fairly easy. Sam had been correct. Lee Sparks had seen Tom Stafford coming an hour before he reached the cabin. Lee knew Tom had to be on official business since he had no other reason to be up there and he would have had to get a map to find the place. He only hoped Tom wasn't bringing bad news.

Lee took the time to close up the cabin and prepare to return with Tom. It was obvious the trip up there was about Sam's condition or it was about the shooting incident. When Tom arrived at the rim of the Hidden Meadow's rim, Lee met him at the top of the log staircase. It seemed to Tom as if Lee appeared out of thin air. Their eyes locked and Tom started first. "Lee, I'm sorry to intrude but..."

Lee cut him off. "Tell me about it on the way down. How is Sam?"

Tom filled Lee in on what happened and how everything transpired. The only thing that made Tom uneasy was Lee's silence. He never said a word. He just listened. When they reached Tom's patrol Blazer Lee said, "Let's go talk to your people. I'm ready."

— — —

Lee Sparks sat in the lobby of the Thompson Police Department while Tom Stafford went to Alban's office and notified Maggie, the department's secretary. "I have Lee Sparks in the lobby." She nodded her head and picked up the phone to call Lieutenant Alban and Captain Fletcher about Lee's arrival. Tom went back to the lobby to retrieve Lee who sat patiently waiting on his return. "Okay, Lee. Fletcher and Alban are waiting for us. Are you ready for this?" Lee frowned at Tom. "Ready for what? They want to know what I know…I'm going to tell 'em."

They stood and walked down the corridor and stopped in front of Fletcher's office. Tom knocked on the door and the usual, "Come," came from within. As Tom and Lee entered the office, they saw Captain Fletcher seated at his desk and Lieutenant Alban standing to his right. Fletcher spoke first, "Mr. Sparks! Thankyou for coming." The captain stood to greet Lee and extended his right hand. Lee didn't return the gesture. Alban remained quiet. Fletcher read the situation and retracted his hand. "Have a seat, please. I expect Sergeant Stafford has explained the reason for this little meeting?" Fletcher looked at Lee in a questioning but concerned manner.

Tom sat down next to Lee and Lee nodded back…first to Fletcher and then to Alban. There was an uncomfortable awkwardness about the room. Finally, Lee spoke. "What can I do for you, Mister Fletcher?"

Fletcher was staring Lee right in the eyes. "Okay, let's get right to it then. Our Site Investigation Team has scoured the area on the ridge above the ravine as well as the area where Sergeant Moody was found. They found a set of boot prints on the ridge that matched those near where Sergeant Moody fell, and Sergeant Stafford filled us in on your sudden appearance on the ridge near the shooter's location after the alleged shooter had been silenced. The evidence shows you were in the area at the time of the shooting." Fletcher paused to allow Lee time to understand that they already knew he had been in the area. "We want to know why you were up there and what you saw."

Lee continued to remain relaxed and stoic as he sat in his chair. In his usual manner, Lee thought about what the captain had just explained, and didn't hurry his response. Finally, Fletcher asked, "Mr. Sparks?"

Lee continued to watch Fletcher and glanced once at Alban standing next to him. Lee calmly replied, "I was out scouting turkey on Opening Day. I was trying to see where the turkey movement was. I figured they'd be spooked by the hunter activity so they wouldn't be too hard to find. I was also kind of interested to see who was out there." Lee paused and added. "That is my business, you understand. I'm a hunting guide." Fletcher nodded but said nothing. Lee continued, "I don't like to hunt on that day since all the guys who don't hunt all year are out there to get their first bird. Everybody seems a little trigger happy." Alban nodded his head and rolled his eyes in agreement. Lee looked back at Fletcher and continued. "I heard a rifle shot…clear as day. Not a shotgun mind you…a rifle. Lee paused then continued, I happen to know the only allowable weapon on Opening Day is a shotgun…20 gauge or larger, so I was surprised. I started over to where I thought the shot came from." Lee paused as if envisioning the scenario in his mind. "Actually, I was pretty close, and heard another rifle shot, as if in answer to the first. That's when I saw someone slumped over a flat rock outcropping…like he had been shooting into the ravine. I ran up to the guy laying across that flat rock and felt for a pulse. There was none." Lee paused, "It looked like the shot came from below because there was blood coming from under his left arm that had been exposed over the left side of that rock outcropping. When I looked down to see where it may have come from, I saw a uniformed warden laying down at the trail entrance. That's when I saw Mr. Stafford here, come out of the wood line into the ravine. I pulled out my binoculars to get a better look and saw it was definitely Mister Stafford. I shouted but he didn't hear me, so I waved my arms in the air to get his attention. When Mister Stafford looked up and saw me, I tried to get down there as fast as I could to see if I could help. I got to where the injured man was and helped Mister Stafford with the bandaging."

— — —

Fletcher had been watching Lee intently as he relived the experience. When Lee finished, Fletcher sat back in his chair and looked over at Alban. Alban showed no reaction. Fletcher looked back at Lee. "Is that all, Mr. Sparks?"

Lee pursed his lips together and nodded in an affirmative way. "Yup. That's it."

Fletcher tried to push Lee, "Did Sergeant Moody know you were up there?"

Lee's face turned serious. "I thought this was about me and what I know. I gave you that."

Fletcher could see Lee was getting impatient and nodded his head. 'You're right, you're right." He paused and continued to lock eyes with Lee. "You were just scouting?" Lee nodded his head again to indicate that he was. Fletcher continued, "That's pretty dangerous on Opening Day, Mister Sparks. Like you said, there are a lot of trigger-happy hunters out there. If I were you, I'd do my scouting before Opening Day from now on."

Lee finally cracked a smile. "That's good advice Mister Fletcher."

Fletcher stood from his chair and turned to look at Alban. He turned back to Lee and said, "Well, Mister Sparks, I'm not real comfortable with your story but there were no witnesses before Sergeant Stafford spotted you on the ridge." Fletcher reached across the desk and extended his hand once again to bid Lee good-bye. "Thank you for taking the time to come in."

Lee stood from his chair and stepped to the side of it, nodded and said, "Are we done?"

Fletcher nodded his head. "Yes, sir. Have a good day." Lee nodded once more, glanced at Alban, turned and walked out of the office.

★★★★

CHAPTER 38

Captain Fletcher's office was quiet for a few minutes after Lee's departure. Fletcher was the first to speak. "I don't believe him! I do not believe Lee Sparks was up on that ridge scouting turkey on Opening Day. Shit! He says he was watching turkey movements?"

Alban was staring at the floor and rubbed his chin. "Well, Cap. You can't discount what he said. There was no one there to say otherwise. We're going to have to take his word for it. At least he admits to being there and came down here without a fuss."

Fletcher looked back at Alban, "Without a fuss? He couldn't have been more obvious in his distaste for being here."

Alban looked up from the floor. "What do you want to do?"

Fletcher paused and said, "We're going to have to talk to Sam."

Alban nodded his head in agreement. "Well, I understand he's home now. We'll give him a day and go have a talk."

Fletcher wore his usual serious face, nodded and looked back down at his desk. "Go to his cabin when appropriate and find out if he knows why Lee was up there."

— — —

Lieutenant Alban waited exactly twenty-four hours before going over to visit Sam. The sun was shining and it was unusually warm for the end of May. He got out of his cruiser and stood for a moment. Alban thought, *Okay, let's get this over with. I don't believe Lee's story either but what difference does it make now? Farmer is dead, and there were no witnesses. Fletcher is walking a thin line trying to prove both of my wardens had an ulterior motive.*

He took a deep breath and started for the cabin when the porch door opened and Peg stuck her head out. "Hey, Gene! Come on in. We saw you pull up. Sam is excited to see you."

Alban climbed the porch steps and walked into the cabin. Sam was sitting in the dining room having coffee. "Hey, LT. How's it going?"

Alban sized Sam up immediately. He was dressed and shaven, hair combed, and appeared completely lucid. His color was good and he wore a good size bandage on his forehead over his left eye. Alban stood in the doorway and smiled. "I see nothing has influenced your love for coffee." Alban walked across the room and shook Sam's hand. "It's good to see you out of bed and in regular street clothes. How does it feel?"

Sam shrugged, "I'm still getting headaches, some worse than others, but the occurrences are dwindling each day." Sam motioned for Alban to sit down.

Alban looked across the table at Sam. "So...when are you coming back? I know the Doc suggested some time off but what do you figure?" Sam turned to Peg who stood across the room leaning against the kitchen counter. She raised her eyebrows in silence as if to say, 'this one is yours.'

Sam cleared his throat and looked at Alban. "I don't know, LT. It's too soon. I can't even think straight right now. I have a lot of things to consider."

Alban's heart sank. *Oh shit. He's gonna' quit.* Alban straightened up in his chair. "Sam, my visit here is two-fold. I came here to see how you are feeling but also to ask about what you knew about why Lee Sparks was up on the ridge that morning." Sam put his hand up as if to say stop but Alban continued. "Please let me finish." Sam dropped his hand. Alban went on, "You did all the right things when your family was threatened by Farmer, and you even warned us that if we didn't do something, you'd be forced to protect your family and property. I get that. Captain Fletcher and I had a talk with Lee Sparks at the PD yesterday. Personally, the Cap and I don't believe him. We think he was your back up." Alban paused for Sam to say something but Sam's facial expression remained stoic. He watched Alban intently. When Sam didn't offer anything, Alban continued. "I have been on your ass since your first day on this unit about having back-up. In this case, I can only surmise about what was going on. I stood outside by my cruiser and realized there is no proof about anything. The only thing that is for sure, is that the problem is gone, the incident is over, and you and your family are safe. It appears no laws were broken… from the evidence we have. Is there anything you wish to tell me at this time?"

Sam looked across the table at his lieutenant and smiled. "You said it all, LT. No laws were broken."

Alban nodded his head and slapped the table with his right hand as he stood up. "That's what I wanted to hear. Get better and get back to work. I'll be in touch." Alban turned and nodded to Peg. "Take care of our boy. We need to get him back soon." Peg smiled back weakly. Alban turned to look at Sam as he left the cabin. "Have a good day."

Once Alban had left the cabin and was out of earshot, Peg glared at Sam with a questioning look. Sam shrugged his shoulders. "He never gave me a chance to say…anything."

★★★★

Printed in the United States
By Bookmasters